THE
PRESENCE
a ghost story

EVE BUNTING

G RAPHIA

Houghton Mifflin Harcourt
Boston New York

www.hmhbooks.com

The text of this book is set in 15-point Goudy Modern MT.

Library of Congress Cataloging-in-Publication Data
Bunting, Eve.
The Presence / by Eve Bunting.
p. cm.
Summary: While visiting her grandmother in California, seventeen-year-old
Catherine comes into contact with a mysterious stranger who says he can help her
contact a friend who died in a car crash for which Catherine feels responsible.
ISBN 978-0-618-26919-8 hardcover
ISBN 978-0-547-48032-9 paperback
[1. Ghosts—Fiction. 2. Guilt—Fiction.] I. Title.
PZ7.B91527 Pr 2003
[Fic]—dc21
2003004034

Manufactured in the United States of America
DOM 10 9 8 7 6 5 4 3 2 1

4500245100

THE PRESENCE

a ghost story

The ghost stood on the church stairs, watching, waiting for Catherine.

He was seventeen years old; he'd always be seventeen, though he had died 120 years earlier. He was as handsome now as he'd been then, unchanged but invisible. Invisible unless he chose to show himself—and he hadn't allowed that to happen too often in all the long, endless years.

The ghost did not like the word for what he was. "Ghost." It made him think of wraiths, of mists and formless forms who moaned and sighed. That was not his way. So he preferred to think of himself as a presence. Once he'd heard an old, old woman say, shivering and clasping her arms about herself, "I feel a presence in this church."

"Of course. You feel God," her younger friend had suggested with a touch of exasperation.

"I am not speaking of God," the old woman said, and the ghost had smiled his invisible smile and thought, She feels me. She is close to death herself, and so she senses

me. He'd laid a feather touch on her old, wrinkled hand and laughed silently when she pulled away and rubbed it nervously on her coat. But she'd given him the word, and it pleased him.

The Presence waits for Catherine, he told himself now.

He was patient because he had nothing but time, time stretching before and behind him. She would come.

There was the sound of voices outside.

He tensed. Would she be right for him? Or another disappointment?

The heavy wooden church door was pushed open.

"Here we are," a cheery voice said. He recognized Eunice Larrimer, Catherine's grandmother.

"It's cold, I'm afraid." He knew that voice, too. Mr. Ramirez was one of the church elders, and he was holding the door open.

"Go ahead, my dear," Mrs. Larrimer said to Catherine.

The Presence leaned forward, holding his ghost breath, clenching his ghost fingers around the scarred church banister.

Catherine! She was exactly the way he'd hoped she would be. Long-legged in her blue jeans, dark hair that tumbled down her back, a face enough like the long-dead Lydia's that he shivered.

"Lydia!" he whispered in a voice that could be heard only by him. Then he closed his eyes, filled with an old, remembered happiness. "Catherine!"

The church my grandmother goes to is immense. It has red sandstone-block walls, turrets, an organ as big as a subway car, and a gallery that curves round and round into the roof shadows.

I'd come to California to spend Christmas with my grandmother because she'd written and invited me to be with her while my mom and dad were in Europe. She'd love to have me, she'd said. And they'd probably thought it would be wonderful for me to get away from home, away from Chicago and all its heartache. Dr. West might even have suggested it. "A change would be the best thing for her," she would have said. She was probably right.

So here I was.

It was my first day, and although it wasn't Sunday, I'd come to the church with Grandma because she volunteers in the office and she refused to leave me alone. She said she'd read in the paper about a fourteen-year-old girl being raped while she was home from school, sick, and

3

that had happened in Alhambra, just a few miles down the freeway. Nothing on earth was going to persuade her that at seventeen I knew all about not opening doors to strangers—which in my case would mean every single person here in Pasadena. That could be her real reason. But perhaps she didn't want to leave me alone in case I started thinking bad and sad and desperate thoughts. And she could be right about that.

So she was in the office with three other volunteers, typing the church bulletin on the church's new iMac. She'd introduced me to her coworkers, and I'd repeated the names to myself so I'd remember them.

Now I was up in the gallery, exploring. The gallery wasn't used these days, since the congregation had shrunk. By the look of it, it wasn't cleaned very often, either.

Although it was December, it was California hot outside. Sun shafted through the big, round stained-glass window, making red and blue ribbons across the dusty pews and floor. Way down below, I could see the pulpit, where Dr. John Miller, the pastor, would preach on Sunday. The church had the hollow emptiness that immense, open buildings have, and there was a smell of old books and mildew and some sort of sweetness—not incense, because I'm fairly sure Methodists don't ever use incense.

I was standing, looking down, fighting a sneeze, when a soft voice spoke right next to me. "Catherine!"

I gave a startled yelp and jumped sideways. "Hey!"

I spun around. I'd thought I was alone, and I was. There was nobody.

But I'd heard my name.

"Who's there?" My voice was wobbly.

I went up a step and looked along the length of the next pew, wall to wall. Empty. But there had to be somebody.

Silence pressed around me. Was someone lying down, along the floor, out of sight? I didn't want to walk all the way up to the last row. What if the someone reached out, grabbed my ankle, and pulled me down? The poor girl who'd been raped just a few miles along the freeway was suddenly very real to me.

"This isn't funny, you know," I said in a shaky voice. "It's bad manners to scare people."

Only silence.

In a rush now, I started toward the stairs that led back down to the vestibule below, and I was telling myself, "You only imagined it, Catherine."

But I knew I hadn't.

And I was remembering how, after Kirsty died, I'd dreamed about her and thought I'd heard her voice whispering, "Help me, help me," the way she had that night, and it had been so real, as real as this. The thought made me feel worse. Was I going wacky again?

I was out now at the top of the stairs, my breath sobbing in my throat, and then I was scurrying down the steps, slipping, my elbows bumping against the banisters. Almost down. Almost down, glancing over my shoulder at the emptiness behind me.

That nice old man, Mr. Ramirez—Arthur, Grandma had called him—was pushing through the heavy front doors. He was carrying an egg-crate tray with five paper cups on it. "I got you a Coke—diet," he said uncertainly. "Is something wrong?"

"I—I—there's somebody up there," I gasped.

He set the egg-crate tray on the bottom step. "For goodness' sake! We can't leave these doors open for five minutes but somebody wanders in off the street. I hope he didn't frighten you."

"A bit." I kept peering up the stairs, not knowing what I expected to see.

"I'll just go take a look," Arthur said.

I grabbed his arm. "Wait!" I swallowed. "Don't you think somebody should go with you?" I didn't add, "Not I," but I was thinking it.

He smiled. His teeth were lovely, big, whit[e] fake, in his little wizened face. "My dear, I'm perfe[ct] capable of throwing somebody out myself. It won't be t[he] first time. It's hard, you know, because we feel so sorry for the homeless. But we've had thefts."

I watched him go. His gray suit was tweed. His shoes were black and pointy. He was tiny as a sparrow, and I could imagine someone crouching at the top of the stairs, giving Arthur one shove and him tumbling to land, splat at my feet.

From inside the office came the cheery hum of voices and laughter. I picked up the egg-crate tray and opened the door one-handed. The noise stopped, and three smiling, rosy faces turned in my direction.

"Hi, there," one of the women said. I think she was Rita. "Didn't I just hear Arthur's voice? Where did he disappear to?"

"He's upstairs. I think there's somebody there. We should go see if he's all right."

"Oh, my!" Grandma jumped up. "You stay here, Catherine." She picked up a fat roll of white paper that looked as heavy as a club. I had to move aside as the three of them rushed for the door. I set down the tray and followed close behind.

the vestibule, there was Arthur

...odness," he said. "Maybe he
...ow."

...u see someone, lovey?" the one called Mau-
...sked me.

"I'm sure I heard a voice . . . or, like, a noise." I let the words trail away uncertainly.

"Oh, goodness, we hear things all the time." Grandma rested her paper roll on the banister. "Animals come in, you know. It's cozy up in the roof space."

"Possums, skunks, raccoons." Maureen pretended to hold her nose. "Oh, those skunks are terrible." She went back into the office and inspected the egg-crate tray. "Arthur? Which one is the real coffee? I can't stand this decaf stuff you all drink."

"The one with the napkin under it," Arthur told her.

I looked over my shoulder, up the wide curve of staircase. They were making it all sound so ordinary. But that *had* been a voice, hadn't it? It hadn't been a skunk or a possum or a raccoon. The voice had spoken my name.

The bottom steps of the staircase were shiny clean.

I pictured kids sitting there, after the service or after Sunday school, keeping them polished with their Sunday pants and Sunday dresses. The dust began about five steps up. I saw two sets of footprints: Arthur's shoes, thin and pointy-toed; and my tennies, with the wide rubber tire tread going up close to the banister, coming down in a series of streaks and skids. In some places his and mine overlapped. But there were just two sets of tracks. Whoever or whatever had been up there was up there still.

TWO

I stood around the office, sipping the drink Arthur had brought. I was glad of the cold Coke. The ice cubes rattling against my teeth were real and solid.

"Sorry for the fuss," I said, managing a smile.

"No problem," Rita assured me. She was a jolly-looking heavy woman with dangling earrings shaped like teaspoons and a bright green sweater with silver jingle bells hanging on the front.

"You're even prettier than your picture." Maureen beamed at me.

Grandma beamed back. "Indeed." She laid a loving hand on my shoulder. "I wonder what's keeping Collin," she asked.

Arthur took a cautious sip of his decaf. "He's probably late getting out of water polo practice. He'll be here."

I rolled my eyes. "Water polo? In December?"

"Yep. It's an outdoor pool, too."

Collin was the pastor's son. He was supposed to pick up Grandma and me and drive us to get the thirty-six poinsettias that had been ordered to decorate the Christmas church.

Grandma leaned across Rita's desk and quirked an eyebrow. "Are you going to get along all right without me this afternoon, Rita?"

"We'll flounder," Rita said. "Since Collin isn't here yet, could you spend five minutes with me, Eunice? It would be a blessing." She appealed to me. "We got this new computer. . . . " Her voice trailed away. "I suppose you're an expert, Catherine. All you young people are."

"Not really."

Grandma peered over Rita's shoulder. "What have you done? You've cut and pasted in the wrong place, Rita. Here, let me at it." She sat in the wooden chair Rita happily vacated.

I took another sip of my Coke and looked around the office. There were two battered desks, one of which held the computer and a printer, a scarred wooden table with papers strewn over it, and four metal filing cabinets with framed photos on top—children and grandchildren, I presumed. There was one of me, smiling, holding Fluffy, our cat. A humungous wall clock ticked loudly.

Grandma squinted at me over the top of her glasses. "Collin won't be long, I'm sure. He's very dependable.

Why don't you take a look around the sanctuary while we wait, Catherine? It's very beautiful."

"I think I'll just stay . . . " I began politely, reluctant to leave the cozy safety of the office.

"I'd be happy to give you a little tour." Arthur slanted a shy smile in my direction.

So he'd be with me. Nice Arthur. Nothing to worry about. I dropped my empty paper cup into the overflowing wastebasket.

Rita gave a sudden shiver and pulled the collar of her sweater higher around her neck. Her long earrings shivered along with her. "Always a draft," she said. "It'll be warm, and suddenly we get this rush of cold air. Old buildings," she added apologetically.

The cold touched me, and I wrapped my arms around myself, noticing the goosebumps rising on my skin. "Brr," I whispered.

"We've stopped saying it's someone walking across our graves," Maureen said. "That's how we used to explain a breath of cold when I was young, in New Orleans. Oh." She stopped, and I knew immediately what she was thinking. She was sorry she had mentioned the word "grave." Sorry if she'd reminded me of things better forgotten.

Grandma would have told them what had happened. She might even have shown them a clipping from the *Chicago Tribune*. A car accident where one teenager had survived but the other one, visiting from another country, had died. They hadn't been found for two days. It was the kind of story the press loved.

"Catherine took it hard," Grandma would have said. "She and Kirsty were very close. The poor child felt so guilty. Heaven knows why."

Heaven knew why. And so did I.

"It's OK," I told Rita. "No need to watch what you say around me. Honest! I'm getting over it."

There was a silence in the office except for the tick of that humungous clock.

"So why don't you and Arthur go have a look at the sanctuary, sweetheart?" Grandma said gently, and Arthur immediately set down his paper cup.

The numbing chill followed us into the lobby.

"The church is made of stone and old bricks," Arthur said. "I think that's why we get these sudden updrafts of cold air. Cracks in the mortar, you know. Last earthquake . . ." He stopped for effect. "Last earthquake, the church got shaken up. We lost part of the steeple. Now we're told we need a retrofit, but that takes money, something we always seem to be short of."

I nodded.

"We're very proud of St. Matthew's," he added. "Last spring it was designated a historic monument."

"Grandma told me," I said.

He pushed open the swinging doors that led into the sanctuary, which I'd looked down at from the gallery. I drew in my breath. What a lovely, serene place. The old oak floor gleamed, the dark wooden pews shone, and the high, high ceiling spread its blessing above us. Stained-glass windows, bright and jeweled, dropped colored patterns on the white walls. I could be at peace here, I thought. This place could soothe my guilt. Instinctively, I lowered myself into one of the pews and closed my eyes.

"I'll just leave you to yourself for a few minutes," Arthur whispered, and I heard him tiptoe away from me, heard the small *whoosh* as the doors swung closed behind him. He knew what had happened, of course. He'd heard the exchange between Maureen and me. But even without that, he would have known from my grandmother how sad and miserable I was, and he had faith in the power of this holy quiet to comfort me.

I tried to push away the thoughts that came crowding into my head. Be at peace, I told myself. But it wasn't going to be that easy, even here. So think about something else—that voice, that unseen person. I shivered and took a quick, nervous glance around the empty sanctuary. Don't think about that, either. OK. Think about Mom and Dad.

"Going to Grandma's will be good for you," Mom had told me.

"I don't think I want to go. I won't be able to be cheerful."

"It's so rotten to be leaving you at Christmas," Mom said. "You know we tried to turn it down. But Dad's firm—well. . . . Anyway . . . " she'd added vaguely. "Dr. West thinks it will be for the best."

Dad stroked my hair. "Grandma won't expect you to be cheerful. You'll be comfortable with her, the way you always are."

My mind jumped to the drive through the early-morning streets of Chicago. Snow piled up, dirty on the sides of State Street. Christmas banners blowing in the frigid wind. The plane. The delay while they defrosted the wings, and then defrosted them again. Grandma waiting for me at the airport in Los Angeles, driving me through the city, where there was no snow, only palm trees and traffic and bustle and sunshine.

Same world, I'd thought. Just different. Better for me for a while.

My legs ached where they had been broken, and I realized I'd slipped onto my knees. I straightened and rubbed at the pain. My chest ached, too, where my ribs had cracked. I concentrated on slowing my breathing.

"Catherine!" Such a soft voice, gentle.

I jerked upright, holding on to the seat in front. Same voice. Same.

My heart began a slow, steady thumping. It must be someone carefully hidden.

"Please, *please* don't do this to me," I whimpered, but my words seemed to fall one by one, soundlessly in the empty space. I clawed my way out of the pew.

The Presence watched her back along the aisle toward the door. He saw the terror in her eyes. Foolish to scare her like that. He'd scared others before her and suffered the consequences. He needed to let her sense him first, let his being fill her slowly.

When he'd spoken to her up in the gallery, her name had spilled from him because there was so much joy in his heart that she'd come at last. He'd told himself he wouldn't say anything more, not yet, not until he'd made her aware.

But when he'd seen her kneeling, her head bowed, her hair draped forward, his feelings had overflowed. He'd seen the tender paleness of the back of her neck, and there'd been this sudden need in him to say her name. He'd given in to that need. He'd been imprudent to rush. No hurry, after all. She thought she was only here for a few days, but it would be more. They had all the time in the world.

THREE

"*H*ey! Watch it!" Hands gripped my shoulders from behind. "Do you always walk backward?"

"No!" I shouted, twisting around.

"Wait a sec! You're all right," the guy said. He let go of me. "Calm down. I'm Collin, and I know you're Catherine. I've seen your picture."

I couldn't focus on what he was saying, and I stared, hypnotized, at the doors into the sanctuary, closed now but swinging slightly where I'd pushed through them.

"I'm here to take you and your grandma to get the poinsettias," he said.

"I was in . . . in there," I told him. "I didn't realize someone else was in the church, too."

"You saw someone?"

I shook my head. "No. Someone spoke." My heartbeat was slowing, but my hands were still clammy with fear. I rubbed them down the sides of my jeans and made myself look up at Collin Miller. He was very tall and skinny. That was all I could take in.

"It's OK, you know. Whoever's in there is probably harmless. I'll go take a look."

They were almost the same words Arthur had said to me as he went up the stairs to the gallery. Uncertainty filled me. I couldn't stand it if I was having some kind of relapse, another bout of that post-traumatic stress Dr. West talked about.

"Sometimes someone comes in the church to pray or rest or whatever," Collin went on.

"Like possums, raccoons, or skunks," I muttered.

"What?"

"Nothing."

"We keep the front door open when there's someone in the office, although we've had our silver candlesticks stolen twice. Manuel, our caretaker, has even had his Sunday clothes stolen from the choir room." He shook his head in mock horror. "But we forgive those that trespass. Church policy."

This time I managed a nervous smile. He was wearing a white sweatshirt with the sleeves chopped off. His hair was straight and blond.

He grinned down at me. "Checking me out?"

I gave a little shrug.

"Only kidding." He seemed a little embarrassed.

"Don't worry about it. I've been checking you out, too."

I shrugged again, not caring what he thought of me.

"So you stay, I'll go," he said, stepping past me to push on the doors.

"No, wait." I moved after him. "I want to come, too." I didn't want to. I didn't even want to be here in the church. But it was good to confront things that terrified you, things that were there and things that weren't. Like Kirsty's whispers. That's what Dr. West had said.

"Don't shy away from what happened, Catherine," she'd said. "Look at it."

"I can't," I'd wailed. "All I see is blood. All I hear are her moans, and her awful, awful silence. I still hear her, and I still hear the silence when I waken."

"Have you ever tried to speak to her?" Dr. West's voice, so quiet and reassuring.

"No. I wake up and I'm drenched with sweat, the bed is soaked. I just about crawl to the bathroom. You don't know, you can't know, how awful . . ," Why do I have to sound so surly? I don't mean to. But Dr. West never takes offense.

"I think one night you and she will talk," she'd said.

I'd smiled sarcastically. "I suppose it's a part of facing

up to things." That's Dr. West's mantra, her solution to everything.

"Yes," she'd said.

So I was going back into the sanctuary now. See, Dr. West? See how I'm trying?

I followed Collin through the swinging doors.

The sanctuary lay filled with time and emptiness, and its old silence.

"Anybody here?" Collin called cheerfully.

My words, repeating themselves, again and again.

No one answered. Again.

"Whoever it was has gone," he said.

I clutched at the side of a pew. "But how could he get past us?"

"Oh, there's a back door. It's supposed to be kept locked, but a lot of the time it isn't." He rubbed his arms. "It's always cold in here when it's empty. Sometimes even when it's full. Right now it's freezing. Are you cold?"

I nodded. Cold and frightened.

Collin waited for me to go out ahead of him, and I was glad to have him between me and the waiting, watching church. I pushed so hard on the door it swung back and bumped my face.

"Easy there. Easy, Catherine," Collin said.

As the doors closed behind us, I thought I heard a sigh and felt a cold breath that stirred my hair.

Grandma stood in the vestibule, waiting, her mammoth-sized purse over her shoulder. "Hi, Collin. We thought we heard you. Well, I see you two have met. Isn't our church beautiful, Catherine?"

"Very," I said. "I remember it a bit."

Grandma smiled. "I doubt that. Catherine was christened here, seventeen years ago," she told Collin.

"Good memory, then," he said. "How come you haven't been back?"

Grandma answered for me. "Oh, I usually go to them." She paused. "Your mom was here, though, Catherine, the summer you went to Scotland by yourself."

I nodded.

"Scotland? By yourself? When was that? Were you—" Collin began.

But Grandma interrupted. Scotland was a dangerous subject, and she knew it. Right now she'd be wondering why she'd mentioned it in the first place. "Are we ready?" she asked briskly. "If I don't get out of here, Rita will have another computer problem and I'll be stuck again."

"My truck's parked right in front," Collin said.

We called our goodbyes into the office and left.

Grandma consulted the slip of paper she took from the outside pocket of her purse. "Thirty-six poinsettias," she muttered as she walked down the front steps. "They should be there and waiting for us. All we have to do is go into the back parking lot, pay for them, and pick them up."

Collin put out a hand to help her into the front seat, but she hopped herself in ahead of him. He gave me a quick lifted eyebrow that asked, "What was I even thinking, wanting to help this lady?"

I sat next to the door as we drove through the Christmasy streets of Pasadena. Fat Santas chimed their bells, and volunteers rattled their Salvation Army buckets. Twinkling lights hung from the sky—and the tall palm trees. The sun shone and shone. It would be dull and gray in Illinois, two hours ahead of California by the clock, steeped in snow and winter cold. Hard to imagine.

I looked down at Collin's bare legs in his cutoff jeans. They were the longest legs I'd ever seen, and his feet in grungy sneakers were gigantic.

"Big as Sheltie shovels," Kirsty would have said.

I stared out the window.

"Here we are," Grandma said at last. "The Garden Shop."

Collin stopped and opened the other door for the two of

us to slide out. I noticed that he let Grandma do her own thing, which she did without any trouble.

The parking lot was as big as a football field, filled with cut Christmas trees, giant pots of chrysanthemums, and holly. The earth and pine-tree smells reminded me of a place Kirsty and I had gone picnicking in the Hebrides, but it had been damp and mushy underfoot there, not hard concrete the way it was here. We'd taken off our shoes and danced, holding hands. We'd draped ourselves with daisy chains.

And why did I have to keep thinking stuff like this? My throat stung. If only I could turn time back to then.

I took a shaky breath, and Grandma squeezed my arm. "OK, sweetheart?" she asked softly, and I nodded.

Collin had wandered a little ways away from us. "I bet those are ours," he called, pointing to a group of poinsettias arranged in three rows. "Twelve, twelve, and twelve. Thirty-six, right?"

"Right," Grandma said. "I'll go pay, and you can load them up."

We stood, waiting. "It's hard to believe, bougainvillea blooming in December," I said, to make conversation. "And what's this?"

"Oleander," Collin said.

Grandma was back. "Those *are* ours, Collin, and I've paid."

I suddenly realized that a very old lady in a wheelchair was staring at me. Her stare made me uncomfortable. I should have been used to this kind of attention by now—I'd certainly had plenty of it—but it still made me cringe. Surely the woman hadn't recognized me from the newspaper picture? That was six months old by now, and in the *Tribune* in faraway Chicago. The nurse who was pushing the wheelchair started to move her on, but the old lady lifted an imperious hand.

"Hi," I said gently.

She kept staring and staring. Her mouth quivered.

I was wondering if it would be rude to walk away when Grandma leaned forward and said, "Why, it's Miss Lottie Lovelace. How nice to see you."

Miss Lovelace had bird legs in white stockings, and her feet on the wheelchair rail were encased in heavy black lace-up shoes. She wore a ton of makeup, bright pink blusher and green eyeshadow. Her high swirl of hair was the color of whipped cream.

"Do you remember me, Miss Lovelace?" Grandma was asking in that loud voice that people use when talking to the very old.

Miss Lovelace didn't seem to hear. Maybe she was deaf? Her little eyes, sunken in folds of old flesh, watched me carefully. The eyes were bright and intelligent.

The nurse hovered uncertainly behind her.

"Miss Lovelace used to go to St. Matthew's," Grandma boomed. "But that was a long time ago, right, Miss Lovelace? Are you still living over on Rosemont?"

The old lady's hand wavered out as if to touch me, then drew back.

"This is my granddaughter, Catherine," Grandma shouted. "She's come to visit."

Miss Lovelace's face twitched. The skin on her cheeks trembled. She crooked a finger, motioning me to come closer.

The nurse bent forward. "Is something the matter, Miss Lovelace?"

Collin, who'd finished loading the plants, came to stand next to us. "Is she OK?" he asked the nurse. "Should I get her a glass of water?"

The nurse frowned. "I think we should just go home. It's not good for her to be upset like this."

Miss Lovelace bent her finger at me, even more urgently.

I made myself lean over her. I could smell a strange mixture of lavender and mothballs and maybe a short, sweet breath of liquor.

"Stay away from St. Matthew's," she whispered. "Run. No as waiting."

"'No as waiting'? What do you mean?" I drew back, fumbling for Grandma's hand.

Miss Lovelace was making faint mewling sounds like a baby about to cry.

"We're leaving," the nurse said firmly. "Say goodbye to your friends, Miss Lovelace."

Grandma and Collin and I stood silently as the old woman was wheeled away.

"What did she say to you, Catherine?" Grandma asked.

I wet my lips. "She said to stay away from St. Matthew's. And something about not waiting. And that I should run."

Grandma frowned. "What on earth did she mean?"

Collin touched his forehead. "I think maybe she's a bit dotty," he said. "Geez, she must be a hundred years old. She probably doesn't know what she's talking about."

I remembered how sharp those eyes had been. Even though her voice had quivered, the old woman wasn't dotty. I didn't believe that for one minute.

The Presence waited for them to come back. It bothered him that Catherine was with Collin Miller. But that sort of thing was inevitable. Soon she would be with no one but him.

He smiled, thinking of the nice surprise he had readied for her when she returned.

FOUR

We were back at St. Matthew's. I was careful to stay close to Collin as we went in and out of the church carrying the plants.

When the flowers were arranged along the altar rail, Grandma stood back, admiring them. "We have the most beautiful midnight service on Christmas Eve, Catherine," she said. "I almost love it more than the one on Christmas Day itself. It's dark inside with the lights turned off. We carry candles and sing carols. You'll see. And of course these magnificent poinsettias line the altar." She began soundlessly counting them, then gave an exaggerated sigh. "I can't believe it. There's one too many . . . thirty-seven. Can't be. I should have noticed."

"Here's one with a blank card." Collin lifted it from among the poinsettia leaves and turned it in his fingers. "Nothing on it. Didn't you say you gave them the printed name cards to put on when you left the order?"

"I did," Grandma said.

Collin passed her the card, and she shook her head and gave it to me.

"What do you mean, blank?" I asked. "Look!"

Collin and Grandma peered over my shoulder, then stared at me.

"I don't see anything," Grandma said, then sharply, "Do you, Catherine?"

My mouth was as dry as sand. I tried to say something, but what would I say? I shook my head. Plain as anything—plain to me—were the words: TO CATHERINE FROM NOAH.

Grandma sighed. "Well, I guess I'll send them a check to cover this extra plant, and we'll just not worry about it."

The card fluttered from my fingers and fell to the oak floor. TO CATHERINE FROM NOAH! Was I losing my mind? Was I seeing words now as well as hearing them? I shivered and stuck my hands in the pockets of my jeans.

"You're cold, Catherine," Grandma said. She took off her white wool scarf and wound it around my neck. "It's freezing in here. We've got to do something about the heating system in this church. Sometimes it's unbearable." She rubbed her hands together. "So, who'd like to walk up to Starbucks and get a cup of latte? I'm buying."

"Man, that sounds good." Collin slapped his long arms

around himself and added, "Especially since you're buying. Let's go."

We were walking back through the choir room when Grandma stopped. "I just thought of something," she said, frowning. "Donna Cuesta . . . poor little Donna Cuesta. Do you remember, Collin? No, of course you wouldn't. You weren't helping with the poinsettias then. Let me think. We had one extra plant last year, too, and . . . " She tapped her finger on her chin. "It's coming back to me now. We couldn't see a name on that card, either. But I recall, Donna looked at it and said, 'Oh, don't worry. It's for me.' She looked so pleased."

We were outside now. The late-afternoon sun was warm on our shoulders. A crow carrying a seed as big as a marble rose heavily into an oak tree.

"Why do you say 'Poor little Donna Cuesta'?" I asked.

"Oh, she always seemed timid somehow. And then, well, she disappeared. Ran away. Her mother was distraught. She said Donna had started wearing a ring on her engagement finger before she left."

The crow dropped the seed and flapped down after it.

"Her mother told us it had two red stones in it," Grandma went on. "It was in an old-fashioned antique setting like a serpent. Sounded hideous to me. I guess Donna was secretive about the ring. I never noticed it. But it obviously came from some fellow. We all decided she'd run away with him. Or maybe they broke up tragically and she couldn't stand being around without him. That kind of thing is always happening in the books I read. And then, of course, the heroine meets someone better." Her voice was cheerful. "In *Lady Margaret's Journey*, the son of the squire dumped Lady Margaret for a vixen he met in a London dance hall and . . . "

I walked between them, not really listening. What had Donna seen on that card that they hadn't? Did it say, "To Donna from Noah"?

A sick feeling washed over me. What was going on?

The Presence had watched them leave for the place called Starbucks. The office ladies went there a lot. He himself had never been because these church walls were his boundaries; the church, his prison. But he knew about Starbucks. He knew a lot about almost everything.

In the office were newspapers to read, a television to watch, a computer that had a search engine from which he could get answers to any questions he had. He'd read the iMac manual and the Teach Yourself the iMac book that Maureen had brought in, and he'd practiced and

worked till he knew the clever little machine by heart.
How could those office women not understand it? So simple. It had opened the entire outside world to him. What
advances there'd been since he was alive!

The St. Matthew's library had books shelved and
cataloged. Politics, history. He'd found his own era. Interesting. But there was nothing about him. Too bad. His
could have been the story of the millennium.

The Presence liked books more than the computer. He
liked the encyclopedia, the feel of the pages. He'd read
through The World Book four times, A to Z. "A is the first
letter of our alphabet. It was the first letter in all the
alphabets from which ours evolved."

"Zygote . . . see Fertilization."

And ghosts. "A ghost, according to tradition, is a
spirit of a dead person that visits the living. . . . Many
ghosts are malevolent. That is, they try to do harm. But
some ghosts are friendly. . . . Ghosts—which are associated with darkness and night—usually end their visits
by dawn."

He'd smiled at that. What did they know? He cared
nothing for day or night. They were both the same. Perhaps, the Presence thought, he'd write a book. Why not? It
would be a bestseller. He'd tell that he could be, had been,

both friendly and malevolent. No doubt he'd be both again.

He smiled to himself. He'd be a ghostwriter.

In the church library were books on God and His plan for humankind. The Presence stayed away from those. He and God were not friends. God had punished him for Lydia with endless years of loneliness. He'd found company for himself a few times, but only temporarily. More than anything he wanted a mate. Someone he could talk to. Someone who'd listen. There might even be love. He had a good feeling about Catherine. Catherine might be the one. And then this ache of emptiness inside him would be gone forever.

FIVE

*C*ollin and Grandma and I walked up to Starbucks. We sat at a small table outside in the sunshine while traffic buzzed by on Colorado Boulevard. Across the street, workers were erecting scaffolding for the Rose Parade on New Year's Day. It would go along here, the floats and the bands, but I would be in the snows of Chicago. Mom and Dad would be back home, too, and I'd pick up living again. If I could.

I was half-listening to Grandma's and Collin's conversation, but I couldn't concentrate. Was it possible that this Noah was the one who had spoken my name twice in the church? Why?

I secretly looked around. What if he was watching me, maybe sitting at one of these other tables? There was an old man tossing crumbs to the birds that flocked around his feet. He was paying no attention to us. A woman with a toddler waited for the kid to finish a tall milkshake. He slurped and blew into the straw. Chocolate froth filled the top half of the glass, and chocolate bubbles rose and popped close to the rim. I turned and gazed along the sidewalk. Only an elderly couple walking their two dogs. Not Noah, I was sure.

"Tell me about being in Scotland," Collin said.

I glanced quickly at Grandma and then said, "It was nice."

"How long were you there?"

"Three months," I said.

"Do you have relatives there or what?" he asked.

I could tell he didn't know anything about the Scotland connection or he would have let it go, would never have started it. He knew about the accident. I'd already sensed that. That must have come in on the St. Matthew's grapevine, or maybe Grandma had told him, but the details weren't there.

"No relatives," I said. "I visited a friend."

His eyebrows were raised, so I added, "Actually, she was my penpal. I met her on the Internet."

Collin grinned. "No kidding. There's probably a word for that. Netpal. Or cyber chum." He took a bite that demolished half of his croissant. "So did she live in a castle in the Highlands?"

I stirred my coffee, swirling the spoon round and round and round. "No. In a house. In a little town called Kilbarcin." There was a river that ran through the village. The low stone bridge that crossed it said "bilded" in 1434. Kirsty and I loved to jump off that bridge into the brown, clear water, cold and sharp as needles. There were pebbles on the bottom, and little fish, sprickly backs, Kirsty called them, that darted around our legs. My eyes were beginning to blur.

"*Your* family went to Europe last year, right, Collin?" Grandma asked quickly. Nice Grandma, changing the subject.

"We did," Collin said. "France, Italy, . . . no Scotland." He leaned across the table. "So did you discover what the guys wear under those kilts?"

I tried to smile. "Never did ask," I said.

Grandma put her hands flat on the table. "I can tell you. They have on underwear, just like anyone else. Lady Fiona, who, by the way, was a perfect lady, mentioned that in passing in the book I read last week. *Her Highland Lover*."

Collin leaned back. "Whew! That's good to know. I've worried about that for a long time."

"By the way," Grandma added, "*Her Highland Lover* was a historical romance set at the time of the Stuarts. Very educational."

There was a faint, faraway ringing. I looked around,

but Grandma immediately picked up her big canvas purse.

"Darn thing," she grumbled. "It's probably Rita, telling me she's lost her template and can't finish the bulletin. She's always calling me about something gone wrong with that computer. But I thought the office people were ready to leave."

We watched while she fished out a cell phone and unfolded it.

Collin grinned at me, and I couldn't help smiling. My grandma, the cyber queen. "Yes?" she asked into the phone. Then she held it away from her and glared at it. "Dumb thing. Why I even have it, I don't know."

From where I sat, I could hear the loud rumble and clicking of static.

"Maybe it's Mom," I said, "and the call's coming in all the way from London. Didn't she say she'd call today?"

"Tonight, I thought." Grandma was banging the phone against her knee.

"That'll really make it sound better," Collin said mildly.

She clicked the off button, but it rang again before she could drop it into her purse.

"Here," she said, and handed it to me. "You try."

"Hello?" I shouted over the static, and suddenly the line was totally clear.

"Catherine? Are you sad?"

The words made my breath catch in my throat. "Catherine?" the voice repeated. "Did you like the flowers I gave you? I want to comfort you."

"Noah?" I whispered.

"Yes, it's Noah. I want you to know that I've talked to Kirsty."

I couldn't breathe.

Grandma was smiling at Collin. "Someone she knows," she whispered happily. "Someone called Noah."

I held the phone away from me, hypnotized by it as if it were a snake.

"Oooh," Grandma whispered. "I guess she doesn't want to talk to this guy."

"Good," Collin said.

Nervously, I put the phone back to my ear, but there was only the loud beating of my heart.

Grandma's voice had changed. "Who was it, child? You've gone as white as milk." She stood up.

Collin stood, too. He took the phone from my limp hand, folded it, and gave it back to Grandma.

I sat there, stunned.

He put his arm around my shoulders. "Was it bad news?" he asked softly.

I shook my head. What *had* it been? What?

"Can we go now?" I whispered.

"Absolutely." Grandma gathered up her purse and scarf. "Is Noah a friend of yours from Chicago?"

I shook my head. I was cold all the way to my bones. What had he meant—he'd talked to Kirsty? When? It had to have been sometime before the accident, of course. That meant he was from Chicago. Why had he followed me here? The awful answer flashed into my mind. Somehow he knew that it had been my fault. Maybe he was Kirsty's dad? A cousin . . . a brother who'd come from Scotland? But I knew her dad and her brothers. They'd never try to scare me like this. Someone who'd known her? Who hated me?

I felt sweat beads break out on my forehead. But he'd said he wanted to comfort me. More likely he wanted revenge. Me alive, walking around, Kirsty dead. And that had been so weird about the static. It was as if he wanted to talk only to me and somehow he knew how to make the line go noisy like that. Some electronic thing. There was a tight band of pain across my forehead.

Grandma took my hand and held it. "It's all right,

sweetie," she said. "Whoever he was, you got rid of him."

We climbed into Collin's truck, and I pulled my seat-belt so tight that it cut into my chest. Safe here between them. Safe.

The Presence smiled as he hung up the office phone. He'd waited impatiently for Maureen and Rita and Arthur to leave. He'd hovered around them, listening to them complain. "Why does it have to be an icebox in here when it's seventy degrees outside?" Rita griped.

He'd gritted his teeth when Maureen said, "Maybe I'll just stay and finish off this bulletin."

Silly old cow. So slow. He felt like leaning down and finishing it for her. But that would never do. Sometimes he wondered what would happen if they found out there was a presence in their precious church. They'd freak out. He'd chuckled. Would they have an exorcism? That might be fun.

But right now all he wanted was for them to get up and go. He'd moved so he was directly behind Maureen and draped himself, weightless, across her back, letting his deathly chill ooze into her body. He'd watched the goosebumps rise on her neck. She'd stood so quickly that some of her papers fluttered off her desk. "I think I'll wait and finish this later," she muttered. Her eyes flickered this way and that. She might seem brainless sometimes, but the Presence often felt she was the only one who sensed something wrong and dangerous when he was around. It amused him. He had to stop himself from shouting "Boo!" into her ear.

He'd dialed the cell phone number that was in the Rolodex the minute they left, hungering to hear Catherine's voice. The thought of her sitting there with Collin Miller drove him wild with anger, even though he reminded himself that Collin wouldn't be in her life much longer.

Was she thinking at all about him, Noah? He'd believed she'd be more happily surprised at his flowers. "Girls love a guy to be romantic," Donna had told him. He'd been romantic with Donna, but in the end he'd had to get rid of her, like so many of the others. He couldn't let her go. What if she told? They'd search the basement. Find his room. Maybe fill it with concrete. Leave him homeless. They might put out a warning. What would it say? Beware of handsome young stranger who promises you secret love? Beware of the ghost? No, better to destroy those who had failed him. It had made him unhappy, but he had no choice.

Way, way back he'd been romantic and charming with Florence Peterson. He'd thought he had her, but early on she'd said, "It's not enough. There's a darkness," and she'd gone and never come back. All he had left now were his paintings of his ladies on the walls of his den. Those and the other unhappy things in the basement that he didn't want to think about.

He'd be romantic when he talked to Catherine. He knew what she needed most was comfort, and he'd promise her that. She needed to get rid of the guilt, and he'd make that happen for her. Lying was one of the skills he'd perfected over the years.

Standing by the window, he watched them walk back, Catherine, her head drooping, her grandmother looking angry, Collin Miller with a stupid, confused look on his face. The Presence didn't think the pastor's son was very smart. Or handsome. The guy was too tall, too loose and lanky. And that hair, like yellow wheat. In his day, they would have called him a "long drink of water." But the idea of good-looking had changed. He'd heard two of the younger girls in church describe Collin Miller as a "hottie." Ugh, he'd thought. The guy always looked scruffy to him, with his jeans cut off at the knees and sweatshirts with the sleeves lopped off.

He himself had always been well dressed and was still—though not in the clothes that had once been familiar to him. Now he had beige pants and a white shirt, thanks to Manuel, who left his Sunday clothes hanging accessibly in the choir room and got very angry the two times they'd been stolen. Manuel's shoes didn't fit Noah, much too big. But then he'd found a nice pair belonging to the Reverend Dr. Miller that fit him perfectly.

He knew he was handsome still. Girls in the past, the ones he'd shown himself to, had swooned over his looks. Several had described him to himself, and he knew he was exactly as he'd remembered, with the same dark curling hair, the dark brooding eyes, the smile that could, as Lottie had said, "make a teapot whistle." But Lottie had escaped him, too.

He couldn't see his own face; the mirrors in the restrooms and the full-length one in the choir room stayed blank when he stood in front of them. But he could feel his features, still firm and tight after all this time. He could sense his body, the muscles hard under the smooth golden skin. It was Lydia who'd first called him Golden Boy. Or was it Alice? Oh, yes, he was handsome. And that was his lure, that and his promises.

The Presence knew he had no soul. It had flown from

his body on the instant of his death. Wasn't that the way it worked? He wasn't going to think about his soul. For him the now was all there was. And soon the now would include Catherine. When that happened, his afterlife would be perfect.

Tomorrow was Sunday. She'd be here in St. Matthew's. He enjoyed playing with her mind. It was part of the chase and would make the revelation even sweeter. Cat and mouse, mouse and cat. Catch and let go.

But he was impatient for Catherine. No more playing. Tomorrow he would introduce himself properly.

SIX

I sat in my room at the desk that used to be my mother's when she was a girl. Outside in Grandma's yard, two squirrels chased each other up a palm tree, then jumped like tiny Tarzans to the branch of an oak tree.

What was happening to me? I couldn't get my thoughts to make sense. Panic swept through me.

"You're not crazy," Dr. West had said.

"I'm not crazy," I whispered shakily. "I'm not." But I *heard* that voice, in the church and on the phone. I *did*.

On a piece of paper I wrote:

1. Noah, who says he talked to Kirsty.
2. Donna Cuesta, who disappeared and who had received a poinsettia from him, as I have.
3. Miss Lovelace, who had warned me about him. Not "No as waiting," but "Run! Stay away from St. Matthew's. Noah's waiting." If he'd followed me here from Chicago, then how did *she* know him? How did Donna?

I'd brought a glass of water upstairs with me, and I took a drink, seeing the shake in my hand, the water sloshing in the glass. There had to be something I could do.

Miss Lottie Lovelace. I needed to find her. She knew Noah, somehow. Maybe he was her son or her grandson, and she knew he was sick and dangerous. That's why she'd warned me. But how did she know he was after me? Unless he'd told her. That didn't seem likely. "Grandma, there's this girl I'm stalking, because——"

No, there had to be a different explanation. Somehow Kirsty was involved. That was the scariest thing of all.

I sat there at my mother's desk, thinking about my mom, longing for her and Dad and the safety of home. But they weren't there. Today they were in London, tomorrow they'd be in Paris. I was here, and for now this was where I had to be.

I could tell Grandma I was sick, which was almost true, and I could stay here, in this house—in bed, even—till it was time to catch my plane home. But Grandma would worry so much. She wouldn't know what to do. Poor Grandma, and she'd been making all these plans for my visit.

And anyway, could I go back home leaving this unsolved? Wondering who he was and what Kirsty had told him. Was she condemning me? But what if she was *absolving* me?

Don't talk crazy talk, Catherine. She can't absolve you. She's dead.

Shivers ran like spiders along my arms.

Grandma was having a reading nap, as she called it. "I just lie down on my bed for an hour or so most afternoons," she'd said. "I start off reading and end up sleeping. Unless there's a bit of good, polite passion to keep me awake. You don't mind if I leave you to your own devices?"

"'Course not," I'd said.

"The garden's nice to sit in, and there are tons of magazines and books. Maybe you'd like to go for a bike ride. My bike's right there in the garage. My helmet, too."

"I'll be fine," I'd reassured her. "I have things to do."

Things like. . . finding Miss Lottie Lovelace.

I went downstairs and got the Pasadena phone book. Back at the desk, I began checking out the Lovelace names. There were only four . . . no L for Lottie, but one N. Could that be N for Noah Lovelace? Could that be him?

I rubbed my hands together to try to stop them from shaking, then dialed. A sleepy, bad-tempered man's voice answered.

"May I speak to Noah, please?" I coughed. Asked again.

"Noah? There's no Noah here." The phone banged down so hard it made my ears buzz.

I'd just have to try the other three numbers, and if that didn't get me anywhere, I'd think what to do next. C. Lovelace. I mouthed the number and dialed.

C. Lovelace. Rosemont Drive. I remembered now. "Do you still live on Rosemont?" Grandma had asked.

"Lovelace residence," a gravelly voice said. I'd heard that voice before. The nurse! Lottie was C—probably short for Carlotta. Or maybe Charlotte.

"May I speak to Miss Lovelace, please?"

"Miss Lovelace is not accepting phone calls today."

She was hanging up.

"Wait," I said quickly, but she was gone.

I checked the address. 434 Rosemont Street. But where *was* that?

There were maps in the side pocket of Grandma's car. I'd seen them on the way from the airport. I ran down to the garage, pulled them out, and unfolded the Pasadena one on the hood of the little VW. There it was—Rosemont Street, seven blocks from here.

Should I go? I could take the bicycle and probably be back before Grandma finished napping. Just in case, I left her a note, *Gone for a bike ride*, and propped it on the dining room table.

It would have been a nice day for a happy bike ride, but my mind churned round and round with thoughts of what I would say, maybe what I would find out. The quiet streets were lined with elegantly decorated homes, Christmas garlands on doors, small blinking white lights. Porches brimming with poinsettias. I'd always liked poinsettias, their bright sparkle and velvety leaves, but now I tried not to look at them. "I want to comfort you." Please, I thought, go away, whoever you are.

Rosemont Street, and here was the house, low and white with dark blue shutters. A spray of greenery and holly curved on the front door.

I propped the bike against the porch, hung the helmet on the handlebars, and rang the bell. Before the first echo died away, the door opened, and the nurse I remembered from this morning peered out at me. "Yes?"

"Hello." I tried to smile. "I'm Catherine. We met

today at the florist's. I wonder if I could speak to Miss Lovelace for just a minute. I promise not to tire her."

"I'm afraid not. She's not at all well." The door was beginning to close.

"Please," I said. "It's really important. I think . . . I think I had a phone call from her grandson."

"Her grandson? She doesn't have a grandson."

"Maybe it wasn't her grandson. Some relative. Noah?"

"Noah?" She looked and sounded puzzled, and the door opened a fraction more.

Behind her I could see the hall. There was a potted plant on a marble stand, an old-fashioned heavy mahogany chest with a brass elephant on top, a large framed photograph on a white wall.

I gasped and put my hand across my mouth. At first glance, I thought I was looking at a picture of me.

"What is it?" The nurse turned to look where I was looking.

"Who is that?" I whispered. "In the photograph?"

"Well, it's Miss Lovelace, of course. When she was young. She—" The nurse turned and looked at me. "For heaven's sake," she said. "She looks a little like you. Actually, very *much* like you."

"Yes." My heart was doing some strange fluttery thing.

The nurse was definitely interested in me now. "You know, when I saw you today, I thought you looked kind of familiar. It's because of the picture, of course. Every day I walk past it, and it's so familiar I never really see it, you know? It's just part of the wall." She looked again at the photograph and then at me. "It is quite astonishing. But, you know, there are differences. It's just that you're the same . . . what would it be? You're the same type."

"Yes," I said again. The word seemed stuck somewhere in my throat.

"Are you maybe family?" The nurse was uncertain. "Miss Lovelace certainly seemed to make some sort of connection today."

"I don't know," I said.

The photograph was sepia-colored, old-looking, taken in full-length profile. Her hair was as dark as mine, bundled up in a loose chignon. Instinctively, I caught my own hair in back and pulled it up.

The nurse was nodding. "Remarkable."

In the photograph Miss Lovelace wore a dark dress with a lace collar. Her head drooped on her slender, pale neck. One hand held a closed book. She was me and yet not me. I felt as if I'd stumbled into some time warp, and I let my hair free again to tumble on my shoulders.

"I tell you what," the nurse said. "I can't let you see Miss Lovelace right now. But I could take your phone number, and she might call you. I'm beginning to think it was seeing someone so like herself that upset her today. She may not want to see you and risk getting upset again. But hold on while I get a piece of paper. Why don't you come inside and wait? I'd like to close the door."

I nodded. "Thanks."

She disappeared, and I took a couple of steps into the hallway. The house smelled of old age and lemon furniture polish. I moved to stand beneath the picture. It was water-stained around the edges, and the paper was cracking on the bottom. A studio name in a fancy golden scroll was in the bottom right-hand corner. I leaned close, trying to see the title of the book she held, but the letters were blurred. I could make out only the word "Life" on the spine. And then I noticed something else. There was a ring on the third finger of Miss Lovelace's hand. A serpent, studded with two stones. That was the description Grandma had given of Donna Cuesta's ring. Had Miss Lovelace known Donna and given it to her? Or was this just another strange coincidence?

The nurse had come back, silent in her white nurse's shoes.

"Miss Lovelace called out to me from her bedroom. I told her you were here, and she got frantic. She tried to get out of bed, but I could see she was dizzy and disoriented. She grabbed my hand and wouldn't let go." The nurse fingered her collar nervously. "She said I have to take her to the bank first thing on Monday. She absolutely has to get something out of her safety deposit box." I could see how frazzled the nurse was. "Whatever it is, it's for you," she said. "You're to come for it Monday. It's very important."

"What could it be?"

She shook her head. "I've no idea. Miss Lovelace is very secretive about some things in her life. Secretive and almost scared."

"Well, if that's OK, I'll come by on Monday."

"Fine," the nurse said. "Come after two. I'm going to insist that she have her nap."

I nodded. "Thanks."

"Secretive and almost scared," I thought. That's exactly the way I feel a lot of the time. It's the way I feel right now.

The Presence hummed "O Little Town of Bethlehem" as he painted, his strokes thick and bold on the uneven gray

crumble of wall. He dipped his brush into the can of
Midnight Black and swirled it to make the perfect color
to match the dark clouds of Catherine's hair. He'd used
Midnight Black a lot.

He stood back and looked along the length of the
wall in his den. There they were: Lydia, Belinda, Eliza
May, Florence, Lottie, who had actually escaped, Alice,
Donna, and now Catherine. Primitive might be the word
for his style, though he rather thought of himself as a
painter like Modigliani. There was a book of his works
in the St. Matthew's library. Yes, they had the same kind
of technique.

He looked again along the length of the wall and
frowned. The paintings of his earlier loves were beginning to fade. His dearest Lydia's hair looked almost
gray. Well, it would be now, of course. She'd be 137
years old, but in his memory she'd always be seventeen,
soft and sweet as maple syrup. Maple syrup over pan-
cakes. That had been one of his favorite taste treats. He'd
loved Lydia's hair. He'd loved to brush it, smoothing the
shine of it.

He walked quickly down to that first painting and
gave her hair a black touchup. "There, my darling," he
said, and went back to the incomplete picture of Cather-

ine. He chose a smaller brush, then dipped it in red paint and carefully outlined the tender curve of her lips.

"Goldarn it," Manuel, the caretaker, had complained to Michael, the gardener. "Someone broke into my storeroom and stole paint again. I've got the place padlocked now, too."

The Presence had smiled. As if a padlock could stop him.

He stood back to ponder Catherine's image on his wall. He'd draw her in the jeans and white shirt she'd worn today. Or maybe he should wait and see what she wore to church tomorrow. It might be a dress. He approved of girls in dresses—old-fashioned, he knew, but so much more feminine. On that last day, Lydia had worn a pink blouse and a skirt that was white with pink roses sprinkled on it. That's how he'd painted her. He hoped that when he took Catherine, she'd be wearing a dress. Maybe it would be silky and soft, the color of the sky. That would be nice. He'd like being with her forever in a dress the color of the sky.

SEVEN

*S*un streamed in my window. I lay in bed, not quite awake, knowing that I was at Grandma's house, sleeping in the room that used to be my mom's. And then I remembered. I sat up in bed, my heart beginning its slow, heavy pounding. Below, in the kitchen, I could hear a Sunday morning talk show on TV. I could smell bacon cooking. Grandma had already started the day.

I got up and put on the robe she had lent me. It was soft and pink and wrapped me immediately in warmth and comfort. "I want to comfort you." Noah. Noah on the phone, in the church. And today, soon, I would be back in St. Matthew's. Would he be there? Would he come up to me, speak about Kirsty? What did he know? I clenched my fists. Stop it, Catherine. Just stop it.

I stood in front of the mirror to brush my hair. No use telling myself not to think about it. That picture yesterday. Lottie Lovelace, who could almost have been me.

What was she going to take out of that safety deposit box? Something about Noah. "Run," she'd warned me. "Run!" In the mirror, my face looked back at me, white and strained and thinner somehow, stretched over my bones. If only I could get through this week.

I went slowly downstairs.

"Good morning," Grandma said brightly. "One egg or two, sweetie?"

"One, please. Can I help?"

"Sit down and eat," she said. "I've been trying to figure out what time it is in Paris. It's the same day, isn't it?"

"Same day," I said, "but tonight."

I unfolded my napkin and stared at the plate of food Grandma had placed in front of me. My stomach heaved. How could I eat this? How could I eat anything?

"It sounds as though those parents of yours are having a wonderful time," Grandma said.

"Yes." They'd called last night. I'd tried to sound normal and happy. What point was there in worrying them? But my mom has some kind of sixth sense. "Is everything all right, Catherine?" she'd asked.

"Fine," I'd lied.

"I don't think so," Mom'd said. "You sound . . . I don't know. Something. You're not doing playbacks, are you?"

"Playbacks" was Mom's word for going over and over what had happened that awful night.

I'd hesitated, not meaning to. "Not really," I said at

last, because this . . . awfulness wasn't a playback, it was a new terror that was somehow connected through Noah. It wasn't worse—nothing could be worse—but it was unknown and frightening.

I forced myself now to take a bite of toast and chew and chew and chew.

Grandma had the Sunday *L.A. Times*, and she gave me the comics section. The colors blurred in front of my eyes.

I nodded, not knowing, not caring.

"So," she added, "that's my signal. Time to get ready for morning service. Aren't you going to eat any more of your breakfast, love?"

"I'm actually not hungry," I said and carried my plate to the sink.

"All right, then. No point in eating when you don't want it. That just puts on weight. I always figure our bodies know best."

I smiled. This wasn't a grandma who made you eat everything on your plate!

I had a quick shower in the little bathroom off my room, made my bed, and got dressed. Black pants, the raspberry red cashmere turtleneck sweater Mom and Dad had bought me for Christmas.

I had a quick thought that I'd see Collin Miller again

today. I'd hardly remembered him through all the terrors of yesterday. But now I remembered perfectly. . . . He'd been so nice. Nice-looking, too, with that tousle of blond hair and that quick smile.

And Noah? What did he look like? I knew absolutely that he would try to contact me today. How could I stay away from him when I wouldn't recognize him? And did I want to stay away? Did I want to keep wondering what he knew and how he knew, wondering forever what Kirsty had told him?

I gripped the edge of the dresser. Of course, I didn't wholly believe he could put me in touch with Kirsty. Still, I had to explore all possibilities. I had to. But Lottie Lovelace had told me to run.

"You look nice," Grandma said when I came downstairs.

"You, too," I told her, and she really did, in a black velvet suit and a white ruffled blouse.

"I like to wear a skirt now and then to show off my legs," she said, extending a leg in sheer black hose. "The legs are the last to go, you know. So why not give them an airing every now and then?"

I grinned. "Nothing on you has gone, Grandma."

She patted my head. "Nice child," she said.

We drove through the Sunday-quiet streets and parked in the church lot. I recognized Collin's truck.

"I guess he can never skip a Sunday morning," I said to Grandma. "Being the pastor's son, I mean."

Grandma made a face. "I guess not."

The heavy front doors of the church were wide open, and I could see that the vestibule was crowded with people. The Sunday before Christmas and probably the whole congregation turning out. As soon as we went inside, I saw Maureen and Rita.

They waved. "Merry Christmas."

"Merry Christmas," I called.

"Hi," someone said, and I spun around, as nervous as a cat, and there was Collin Miller.

"Everything all right?" he asked, and I knew he'd seen how jittery I was.

"Fine," I said. "Perfect."

"Will you be OK, then?" Grandma asked. "I just have to dash in the office for a second. Collin will keep you company."

"I have to leave, too, for a minute," Collin said when she'd gone. "My dad wants me to go in back and check the tree lights. Do you want to come with me and watch me be a genius at work?"

"Not really," I said. "I'll wait here. Grandma might come back and wonder where I'd disappeared to. She won't be long."

When he'd gone, I looked around at the people standing in clusters, talking in loud, happy voices. "Is Santa going to be good to you this year?" "Marlene won't be home. She's going to her fiancé's parents' for the holidays." "I know how that is. You have to share." "I got Bill a sweater. Seems like I always buy him a sweater." Everything normal and ordinary.

A woman standing close to the door was looking intently at me. I smiled uncertainly, but she didn't smile back.

Now she was coming toward me.

"I'm sorry to stare at you like that," she said. "I'm Connie Cuesta. My daughter, Donna, is . . . " She stopped and bit her lips. "My daughter, Donna, has left home. I'm not sure where she is right now."

"My grandma mentioned her," I said. "I'm sorry." Why was the woman telling me this?

"The thing is . . . " She seemed to be searching for words. "The thing is, you remind me so much of her. From the back—same hair, same height. When I really look at you, of course . . . of course you're not Donna. But just for a minute."

"I look like her?" I asked nervously. I looked like Miss Lovelace, too, when she was my age.

"You do look like her. Of course, I think I see her in every beautiful young girl. But . . . wait a second." She opened the purse she was carrying and pulled out a leather photo holder. "This is Donna." There was a sudden catch in her voice. "And this." Before I could open the photo holder, she handed me a long postcard that had a brightly colored advertisement for carpet cleaning on it.

"Other side," she said.

I turned it over. There was a postage stamp–sized picture on it, a girl with long dark hair. She stared out at the camera, a small smile on her face.

"High school yearbook," Mrs. Cuesta said. Above the picture, in heavy black print, were the words HAVE YOU SEEN THIS GIRL? In smaller print, underneath, it said: *Name*: Donna Lee Cuesta. *Age*: 16. *Height*: 5 ft, 5 in. *Weight*: 126 pounds. *Hair*: black. *Eyes*: brown. *Sex*: F. *Date missing*: 2/25/2002.

My hand was shaking. It could have been a description of me. At the bottom of the card it said CALL 1-800-THE-LOST.

The Lost! They were the saddest words I'd ever heard, echoing and echoing in my head like some faraway gong.

"These went out in the mail. It's an advertisement, you see. But the company gets to mail them free if it does this public service." She spoke in short, jerky sentences, as if she couldn't hold onto her thoughts.

I nodded. How many times had I seen postcards like this, and I'd just given them a quick glance and tossed "The Lost" out with other junk mail?

"This is a better picture of her," Mrs. Cuesta said. "You can really see that she does look like you." She touched the photo holder gently.

I opened it, and there she was, serious now, gazing out at me. Donna Cuesta. Head and shoulders only. No chance to see if she was wearing the serpent ring. She did look a little like me. Same type.

Who had said that before? Lottie Lovelace's nurse.

My hands were suddenly so sweaty they left finger-prints on the dark red leather.

I handed it back. "I'm sorry, Mrs. Cuesta." Sweaty hands and a mouth that felt as dry as bone. "Have you . . . have you heard anything at all from her?"

She tucked the picture carefully back into her purse. "Nothing. She just vanished. And I don't know why I'm telling you all this. I guess because you reminded me. Just looking at you. And to be honest, I do bother people a lot with my story. Maybe one of them has seen her and forgotten. You know, strange things happen?"

And at that minute I saw him. He was sitting on the stairs, watching me. He wore a white shirt, the long sleeves rolled up above his wrists. His dark hair curled over his collar. When he smiled at me, there was so much brilliance and light, it almost took my breath away. There was such a grace about him, such an ease as he lounged there, long legs stretched out in front, one arm casually draped across the banister. He was definitely and absolutely the most handsome man I'd ever seen in my life. And definitely and absolutely I knew he was Noah.

Mrs. Cuesta was folding the "Missing" card along the crease and tucking it back in the side pocket of her purse.

I touched her hand. "Mrs. Cuesta? The guy sitting on the stairs. Do you know him? Who is he?"

She turned to look, turned back. "On the stairs?"

"Yes." Over her shoulder, I could see him, still sitting, still smiling.

"Do you mean the man standing by the table?"

"No," I said nervously. "On the stairs."

Collin was weaving his way toward us. Before she could answer, he said, "Hello, Mrs. Cuesta. How are you?"

"Fine." She gave me a puzzled look and drifted away.

"Too bad you weren't there to see the way I took care of those Christmas tree lights," Collin said. "First there was a bang. Then a lot of smoke." He spread his hands. "And now a tree without any of those flashing, irritating red and green bulbs. Much more peaceful, right?"

"Right," I muttered, watching the guy who was maybe Noah—who was definitely Noah—coming in our direction. I moved a step closer to Collin.

"You know the person who gave me the flowers," I whispered. "I think he's on his way to talk to us."

"Where?" Collin peered over the heads of the jostling people. He waved to some, and called out hello and Merry Christmas. "Where is this guy?" he asked. "Would you like me to inquire if his intentions are honorable?"

"No," I said, because by then he was standing next to us, saying to me, "Catherine. I'm Noah."

"Yes," I whispered.

"What?" Collin asked. "You *do* want me to ask?"

Neither Noah nor I answered. "It's nice to meet you at last." Noah smiled that dazzling smile.

Collin turned his back on him and said to me, "I bet your grandma's checking her e-mail. That grandma of yours gets more e-mail than anybody else I know, even my dad—and he gets plenty." He turned up the collar of his jacket. "Did it suddenly get cold in here?" Why was he being so rude to Noah, ignoring him like this?

"By the way, Catherine," Noah said. "My last name is Vanderhorst. Noah Vanderhorst." He gave me an old-fashioned kind of a bow, and for a minute I thought maybe he was going to kiss my hand.

"I need to know what you know," I said. "Are you a psychic or something?"

"Of course." Collin grinned. Did he think I was talking to him? "I see things," he went on. He closed his eyes. "Now I see us, you and me, at *The Nutcracker*. Tonight. In the Civic. And I see us having burgers first in Hamburger Heaven."

"I'm not a psychic," Noah said to me as if Collin hadn't even spoken. Almost as if he was used to being ignored. "I'll explain. Not now. Later. But I can arrange for you to talk to Kirsty yourself."

What was going on here? Collin and Noah didn't speak to one another—didn't even seem to see one another.

I was shivering all over. I bit at my knuckles. If I could really talk to Kirsty. If I could ask her forgiveness. If she could take this awful guilt away from me.

I had a flicker of fright. Could I really be taking this all seriously, as if it was really going to happen? But there *were* people, weren't there, who could talk to those on the other side? That's what they called it, "the other side," as if it wasn't so far away and unreachable. As if they were just on the other side of a door or a wall, or just in the next room. For a second I seemed to see Kirsty, laughing that belly laugh of hers, saying, "Come on, wee girl. You mean to say you've been all worried? *Dinna fash yersel'!*"

"Oh, please," I breathed.

"Catherine. Catherine. What's wrong?" Collin asked. "You're thinking sad thoughts, aren't you? You're freaking yourself out." He took my hand, but I pulled it away.

"Let's go find your grandma," he urged.

Noah leaned closer. "Come back this afternoon. Meet me here in the lobby. Come when your grandmother is having her nap. She has one every day, right?" He flashed another smile. "I've heard her mention it to Rita and Maureen. Her reading nap."

I nodded.

"I'm going to get your grandma," Collin said.

"All right." I didn't care. I was only interested in the most important question I still had to ask Noah. I waited till Collin had gone, pushing himself quickly through the laughing, talking people. The noise was beginning to hurt my head. I took a shaky breath. "Noah? Does Kirsty forgive me?"

"You can ask her yourself," he said.

Then Grandma was beside me, her face pale and worried. "Catherine? Collin says you're not . . . " She paused. "He says he thinks you're not feeling well."

"I'm fine," I said and turned toward Noah.

But Noah was gone.

The service was probably beautiful. Old hymns, old carols. I didn't hear much of it. The Reverend Dr. John Miller looked so much like Collin. His words were soft and warm, and they soothed even though I wasn't listening to the sense of them. I thought that if someone was ever in trouble, he or she could go to Dr. Miller. He would try his best to help.

The Christmas tree stood serenely in front of the largest of the stained-glass windows. It was decorated with paper and straw ornaments that looked as if they'd been made by children. We used to do that, I remembered, when I was little. I always made the straw donkey. No lights on the tree.

I tried to concentrate. Had Collin Miller asked me to go

out with him? To something? *The Nutcracker*, that was it.

There was a Nativity scene in front, Mary's robe, as blue as the Pasadena sky, and behind it, the row of poinsettias glowing scarlet in the candlelight. Which poinsettia was mine? From Noah?

Where was Noah? I turned my head cautiously, but I couldn't see him in the overflowing church.

Next to me, Grandma sang in a low, tuneless voice. Every now and then she'd touch my hand or my arm and smile encouragingly. She'd be hoping and praying that I wasn't starting to go crazy again. I'd sensed her thoughts and Collin's, too, but they didn't make much sense to me. Maybe asking Noah if he was psychic had upset them. I guess getting involved with a psychic alarmed people. I'd never thought about it before. But I wasn't alarmed now. Just filled with hope.

When Dr. Miller had given the pastoral prayer, I'd kept my head bent and prayed for myself. That I would be allowed to talk to Kirsty. That she would be forgiving. And then, from somewhere, a prayer of my childhood slid into my mind:

Keep me safe, O Lord, I pray,
Stay beside me through the day.

I clasped my hands along the back of the pew in front. "Stay beside me," I whispered. "Keep me safe."

The Presence listened to the service, hummed along with the music, watched the congregation, watched Catherine. He loved the way her hair streamed down her back. He'd brush it the way he'd brushed Lydia's. Alice's, too. But he didn't want to think about Alice. Catherine's lips matched the sweater she wore. He loved the sweet, pure curve of her cheek.

She wasn't joining in the hymns. She kept her head bent even after the prayers were over. She was thinking about him and about this afternoon. Of course she was. He felt wonderful. He'd seen her talking to Donna's mother, and for a few minutes he'd been nervous. But what was there to be nervous about? Nobody knew.

The fourth Advent candle had been lighted, and it glowed with the other three, its flame bright and steady in front of the altar. The Presence didn't like candles. He didn't like fire of any kind. Sometimes when it was cold, Manuel lit the big old-fashioned boiler in the basement, and it roared and flamed before it caught and settled into its low rumble. Whenever the Presence saw Manuel coming with the long taper, he crouched low in a corner and put his hands over his face.

Often he pondered fire. Why did it scare him? He thought it was because he knew about the flames of Hell. He'd never be going there or anywhere. So why did the descriptions terrify him? He'd decided that the people he'd lived with when he was little, the couple who had taken him from the orphanage, had preached so much about eternal damnation and the bottomless fiery pit that it was burned into his brain. Well, they were probably there now themselves.

Strange how those early days came back to him so clearly. His "parents." Mrs. Evangeline Tibbs, with her hair screwed into its tight scraggle of bun. Mr. Hubert Tibbs, in his dark suit with the stained three-button waistcoat. Oh, yes, when the Presence had strangled Lydia, they'd wept and wailed, saying how they'd tried so hard with Noah, but how they had suspected, been afraid deep down, that the woman who'd given birth to him, who'd given him up, had left her stain upon him. They hadn't cried at his graveside, not even when the minister had said that God forgave Noah his terrible sin and they must, too. They hadn't. And, as it turned out, neither had God.

The Presence felt anger rise hot inside him when he thought of the Tibbses. Well, they were gone and he wasn't.

Someday he'd tell Catherine all about them. She'd listen and sympathize. She'd take his head in her lap, and he'd tell her about Lydia. But not right away. "Lydia didn't love me enough," he'd say. "What else could I do?"

Catherine would understand.

*A*ll through lunch, I could tell that Grandma was anxious. Collin had told her that I was upset, that he didn't think I was feeling well. So now she was wondering if I was going to go off into one of my episodes, like the ones Mom had worried her about.

For lunch we'd fixed a salad with pears and walnuts and blue cheese that was probably delicious. Grandma piled a lot on her plate. I had no interest.

"Collin tells me you and he are going to *The Nutcracker* tonight." She passed me the basket of crackers, and I took one and pretended to nibble at it. "That'll be fun," she said. "One of my earliest and nicest dates was with a boy called Norman Ferraro. We went to *The Nutcracker* at the Civic. At intermission, he bought me a glass of punch, out on the patio. We sat at one of the little folding tables, and it was so cold. I didn't have a wrap." She sighed. "But I would have sat out on top of the North Pole to be with Norman Ferraro."

I smiled. "I'm not sure if you can actually sit on the North Pole," I said, and Grandma waved an airy hand.

"Whatever."

I sensed she was talking to keep my mind occupied so there would be no space or time in it for "playbacks." Mine, she knew, would not be the nice kind, about Norman Ferraro and *The Nutcracker*, but about blood and moaning and death.

"You'll have a terrific time," she went on. "Collin is not Norman Ferraro, but I suspect he'll be exciting and maybe even a little bit daring. That's good in a beau."

I stared into space. By that time, I'd have talked to Kirsty. By that time, my whole life might have changed. For the worse or for the better? Oh, it had to be for the better.

Grandma's table was in front of the French windows that led to her little garden. Sun poured in and lay in squares of light and shade on the green placemats and red-and-green-checked napkins. Outside, a blue jay hopped from the patio to the chair and cocked its head at us. Everything so normal. Was Kirsty able to see me now?

Was she waiting, as I was, for the chance to make things right between us again?

I glanced surreptitiously at my watch and folded my napkin. "Why don't I clear up and you can start your reading nap?" I suggested.

Grandma gave me a serious, questioning look. "I'm not in the mood for reading today. This new book of

Stella Carrington's is not up to her usual standard. It's like she's run out of luscious ideas. Her heroes all look alike, tall, dark, and handsome. I'd like to read about a blond hunk for a change." She put the lid neatly on the butter dish. "I was thinking we could go down to the Huntington Gardens and have a walk this afternoon. It's beautiful at Christmastime," she added.

I paused on the way from the table with our used plates. She was going to keep a loving eye on me. My heart dropped. How was I to get away? "The only thing," I said hesitantly, "I thought I'd go for a run. You know, when I'm . . . " I paused. "When I'm confused or maybe down about something, a run really helps me. I can sort things out. Dr. West told me that that's a medically known fact, something about endorphins. . . ." I let the words trail away. "I thought maybe, while you were reading . . . "

Grandma smiled happily. "A run is a great idea. I'd come with you, but I'm more of a walker than—"

I interrupted. "Alone is better."

"I imagine it is, honey," she said softly. "And you won't get lost? You'll remember how to get back here?"

"Absolutely. I might even stop at The Juice Place and buy myself a fruit drink."

"Perfect. And I'll try Stella Carrington again. Maybe she'll get better in the next chapter."

We smiled at each other. "All right, now." Grandma took the salad bowl to the sink. "You get started. I'll finish here."

"Thanks."

I ran upstairs, changed into sweats and running shoes, tied my hair back. In the mirror, I saw myself, pale, big-eyed. I smoothed on pink lipstick and rubbed blusher into my cheeks. Never in my life had I put on makeup to go running. But never in my life had I been going to meet a dead friend, and Noah.

"Be careful, lovey," Grandma called after me.

"I will."

I ran along her street, past the sleepy Sunday afternoon houses. A dog came with me for a half a block, then turned back. It was hot, but cool under the trees. In the distance, the tops of the San Gabriel Mountains were dusted with snow.

Now I could see St. Matthew's. Instinctively, my running steps slowed. Was I getting myself into something not only frightening but also dangerous? I was going into this church, which was presumably empty except for Noah and a dead spirit. Did I want to be like one of those mindless girls in old Hitchcock movies who went up and opened forbidden attic doors when they knew perfectly well that something obscenely awful was waiting for them in there? I'd always laughed, embarrassed for the girls, and said, "Oh, give me a break!" Was that the kind of stupid thing I was planning to do now?

I stopped and leaned against a tree trunk. What did I know about Noah anyway? I knew he'd had a grand-father, or maybe a great-grandfather, also called Noah, who had somehow terrified Miss Lottie Lovelace. She'd liked the grandfather once, enough to wear his ring. She'd looked like me. I suspected maybe this Noah—my Noah—had had a love affair with Donna Cuesta, who also looked like me. He'd given her the ring, which obviously had obviously been handed down. But something had happened, and Donna Cuesta had run away to become one of the Lost.

I began walking slowly toward St. Matthew's. For some reason, Collin didn't like Noah. He hadn't even ac-knowledged his presence this morning or spoken to him. Probably he didn't like psychics. Noah had said he wasn't exactly a psychic. Perhaps he considered himself a medium. A "channeler," channeling dead people's thoughts into those of the living. I'd heard one interviewed once on TV. Creepy!

I began to shiver, big rippling shivers that ran along my body like waves along the sand. Probably Collin didn't go for channelers, either. Come to think of it, Donna's mother had ignored him, too.

I stopped again. I was in the shadow of St. Matthew's now. Still time to turn around and run back to Grandma's. But then . . . but then I'd never have another chance to maybe get beyond this awful happening. I'd live always wondering if Kirsty had absolved me. Wasn't "absolved" the word they used in church? And what bad thing could happen anyway? I would be in St. Matthew's, in the middle of a city, with someone I'd met in this church, this morning, someone who was almost certainly one of the congregation.

I stared up at the massive stone building. Birds circled its turrets.

Two small boys holding skateboards rested against the front wall, watching me curiously.

"Hi," I said.

"Hi."

The church looked closed and empty. Weren't the doors always kept locked? Suppose when I went up the steps and tried the doors, they were locked and I couldn't get in? That would make the decision for me. Except there was still that back door that was supposed to be kept closed but might be open. My feet felt weighed down as I climbed, every step an effort.

I turned the handle, and the heavy carved door creaked wide. And there—in the vestibule—was Noah, smiling that luminous smile, making that little old-fashioned bow.

"You did come," he said.

"You thought I wouldn't?"

"I thought you would. Let's go in the sanctuary. You need to catch your breath. I watched you running and then slowing after you came to the corner. I decided you were tired."

"Not really." There was nothing wrong with him watching me, out in the open, on a public sidewalk. So why did I feel a little squeamish, as if he were a Peeping Tom? Ridiculous of me.

Oh, it was cold in the sanctuary. This must be the coldest church in the whole world. My running sweat was turning to icicles on my body. The air smelled of pine, of Christmas trees, of chill, of Christmas. The thirty-seven poinsettias glowed fiery red in the light from the stained-glass windows.

We sat in the back pew. "Here." Noah took a knitted

blue comforter from the seat and draped it around me. "I was ready for you. This is Rita's. She won't mind."

I snuggled into it. "Do you work in the church?"

"As little as possible," he said and smiled.

I listened to the absolute stillness. It was frightening somehow, ominous. "Should we sit outside instead?" I suggested. "It would be warmer."

Noah frowned. "No. I can only make contact inside the church."

"You're going to . . . make contact with Kirsty today?" I was stammering.

"Catherine . . . " Noah reached out and put his hands over mine where they clutched the blanket, and I felt raw glacial cold shoot from my fingertips to my shoulders.

I yelped and jerked away, the comforter dropping in a pile at my feet. "Oh, oh, sorry," I whispered. "How rude." I rubbed my arms to try to get some feeling back into them. "It was just—I was so startled. My goodness, you should have a jacket or a sweater. . . ." My words trailed away as I retrieved the comforter.

Something had come over his face, some dark displeasure, a shadow that disappeared when he saw me looking at him.

"Don't be embarrassed," he said. "I have a circulation problem. But you know what they say—cold hands, warm heart."

I wanted to reach out and take them in mine again, to make amends for hurting his feelings, but there was something repulsive in the touch of them, and I couldn't make myself do it.

"About Kirsty," I said quickly. "I've thought of nothing else since this morning." I felt my eyes well up. "I'm scared, you know. And excited. And . . . " I swallowed back the tears. "And just hoping."

"Poor Catherine." Such softness in his voice. "I talked with Kirsty this morning. I told her you were coming."

I squeezed myself small in the comforter. Security blanket, I told myself stupidly. "What . . . what did she say?"

"She said she wanted to talk to you about the party. The one you were coming home from when she was killed."

Killed! The awful baldness of the word.

I felt dizzy. "Oh, God," I moaned. All of it, the awfulness of that night, rushed back to swallow me, and now these words from a dead girl, my dead friend.

"Are you all right?" Noah reached out for me, but I

shrank away, not meaning to, just sick and frightened. I stared up at the stained-glass window, Christ surrounded by the little children. FOR OF SUCH IS THE KINGDOM OF HEAVEN.

"It's all just such a shock," I whispered.

"I know. It will be easier in the lounge."

I stared. "Where?"

"Oh, the Cambria Lounge, downstairs. It's half—sitting room, half—rec room. But it's not used much anymore." He smiled that dazzling smile. "It's quiet. We won't be disturbed. I told Kirsty that's where we'd meet."

"It's quiet *here*," I said quickly. Here I knew. From here I could run if I had to. I could get to the door that led to the street.

What was the matter with me? Why did I think of running? This was what I wanted, this chance. To come today was my own choice. "Did she say anything else?"

"She said, as soon as I call her, she'll come. She said you're still her wee banty hen."

My mouth felt numb, as if I'd had a shot of Novocain. "Banty hen," I whispered. "That's what she used to call me." And nobody else knew that name, not Noah, for sure. Maybe I'd told my mom. Maybe.

He spread his hands, those frozen hands. "Shall we go down to Cambria?"

He held my arm and helped me up, helped me to walk. I stumbled up the side aisle beside him, tripping on the comforter, my legs like wood, cold radiating up my arm from his touch, numbing my shoulder. Banty hen! Wee banty hen!

"Catherine? Is that you?"

I hadn't heard the swing doors from the foyer open behind us. But Noah must have heard, because when I turned to look at him he'd disappeared, hidden himself maybe behind one of the stone pillars.

I swung around. "Dr. Miller?"

He was standing just inside the doors, the pastor, Collin's father.

"Are you all right, my dear?" I sank into one of the pews, the comforter bunched in front of me, watching him walk toward me. "Is your grandmother with you?"

I shook my head.

"Ah." He smiled. "You came back to church this afternoon to just sit and think about things. Is that it?"

"Yes." Where was Noah? Panic filled me. What would happen now? Would Kirsty think I wasn't coming? Would she leave and never give me another chance?

I rose, swaying a little, and Dr. Miller put an arm around my shoulders, so warm, so soothing. "Don't let me chase you away, Catherine. I came back this afternoon myself for almost the same reason. Sometimes I need to have quiet and the comfort of the church. But there's enough room in God's house for both of us. You take your time."

He smiled at me, then walked slowly toward the altar.

How long would he stay? Would Noah come back? I slid forward onto the kneeling stool and put my head down on my folded hands. It wasn't so cold now. Not nearly so cold.

If Noah didn't come back, how could I get in touch with him? Could I call the church number? Would he be here? Did he stay here? I knew so little about him.

I pulled one of the little registration envelopes from the pew in front and took the stub of pencil from its holder. "*I have to see Kirsty*," I wrote. "*Tomorrow. Here.*" I slid it back among the other envelopes so that it stuck up, then closed my eyes and talked to God about Kirsty. "I don't know if what I'm doing is right or wrong. But you are an understanding God, and if it's wrong, I know you will forgive me."

Dr. Miller was still kneeling at the altar, the row of poinsettias scarlet in front of him. I stood quietly, but he heard and turned around. "Are you ready to leave, Catherine?"

"Yes." I folded the comforter and left it on the pew.

"I'll walk out with you and lock up," he said. "I'm glad you were able to get in when you needed to. But the building is supposed to be kept locked when no one is inside. I don't know why it was open."

Because Noah opened it for me, I almost said. But clearly Noah didn't want the pastor to know he was here.

Dr. Miller and I stood together in the foyer.

"Do you believe people who are dead can come back and speak to you?" I blurted out the words, aghast when I realized what I'd said.

He touched my cheek with gentle fingers. "I believe, if you open your heart, anything is possible," he said.

He stood at the top of the steps, and when I was almost at the corner, I turned and he was still there, watching over me.

The Presence hummed as he walked along his wall of ladies. Every now and then he'd stop to talk to one of them and share his good fortune.

"At first I was furious that the pastor came and spoiled it all," he told Florence. "I was just about to get Catherine down here." He paused. "You haven't met Catherine yet, but you'll like her."

Florence looked back at him with her dark, indifferent, dead eyes.

"I almost had you, my lovely Florence. We went together to the brink, but you pulled back." He noticed a speck of dirt on her painted skirt and bent to rub it away. "You were foolish. We could have had a good afterlife together here in St. Matthew's. I find I have just about all I need here. Except . . . I don't have the one thing I want more than anything. A soul mate to truly love and cherish me. Do I have the right to a soul mate when I don't have a soul?"

He moved along to talk with Eliza May. "Today worked well for me. Lovely Catherine wrote a note." He took it from his pocket, carefully unfolded it. "See?" He held it up in front of Eliza May's vacant eyes. I have to see Kirsty. Tomorrow. Here.

"Like the rest of you, my loves," he said pityingly, "poor Catherine is a bit unbalanced. Her parents know, her doctors know, her grandmother knows, and the good pastor knows. None of them will be too surprised at what happens. Shocked, devastated, but not surprised." He looked back along the line of paintings. "Your own disappearances were not unexpected. You were despondent and depressed, poor darlings. I was sorry for all of you. With me, each of you could have had a better life. But not one of you loved me enough. Always frightened. Always trying to escape. I couldn't let that happen. Someone might have believed your incredible stories. And then what?"

He lay down on his folding cot, the one Manuel had once slept on in the old unused rec room where he stayed for a while to save on rent. It always made the Presence laugh to remember how terrified Manuel had been when he heard the organ playing itself in the middle of the night. "Twinkle, Twinkle, Little Star."

The Presence often played in the night hours, pulling out the stops and banging discordant chords that thundered around the church. "Magnificent!" he'd shout. "Catatonic!" He loved words, even ones that made no sense.

That night was the end of Manuel sleeping here to save money. After that he became a caretaker.

The Presence picked up the book that waited for him at the side of the cot. The Secret Garden. He loved that book. He'd read it and reread it. The little girl, lonely as he was, who'd found a secret garden filled with flowers. He missed gardens. The only flowers he saw were through a window or in the stilted arrangements that adorned the altar on Sundays. Sometimes he took one or two of those and brought them down here. It was so cold in his den that they lasted for a long time, but not forever. Nothing lasted forever—except himself. Catherine wouldn't, either. Time wouldn't stop for her the way it had for him. She would always be human. She'd get old and die. That seemed so sad and unfair. But they'd have many years together before that, wonderful, loving years. And perhaps, perhaps, she would become a ghost, too. Perhaps their great love would keep them together after her death. He'd read a book by Charlotte Brontë called Wuthering Heights. In it, the love of Heathcliff had brought his beloved Cathy's ghost to him after she died. Cathy! Catherine! It would happen. Wasn't his love for his Catherine as strong as Heathcliff's?

He opened her note again. The "wee banty hen" was what had convinced her. The pet name was one of the things her grandmother had revealed privately to the pastor, kneeling at the altar rail, seeking comfort. The Presence had knelt beside her, listening intently.

"They'd been to a party," the grandmother had said. "Her best friend, Kirsty, was visiting from Scotland. She was driving. Kirsty was killed. Catherine lived. For some reason, she blames herself."

The grandmother had started sobbing, and the Presence had felt like putting an arm around the old lady's shoulders and consoling her himself. "The girl, Kirsty, used to call Catherine her 'wee banty hen,'" the grandmother said. "I think it's a Scottish endearment. Catherine's mother told me that Catherine often wakes in the night saying she's heard Kirsty asking her, 'Why did you make me do it?'"

"Do what?" Dr. Miller asked in his gentle soothing voice. "Do you know what Catherine made her friend do, Eunice?" And the grandmother had wiped her eyes. "No, we just don't know."

The Presence touched the folded note to his lips. "Soon, my wee banty hen," he whispered. "You will tell me, and I will comfort you."

*T*here was an e-mail from Mom and Dad. It was raining in Paris, but they said it was wonderful anyway. They'd spent the day at the Louvre and would probably spend part of tomorrow there, too. There was so much to see. Mom's biggest surprise was that the *Mona Lisa* was so small. She'd expected it to be bigger. But it was truly exquisite. They hoped Grandma and I were both well. They missed me so much, and although they were loving their trip, they were longing to get home and see me. Only four more days. They were already counting.

"We'll send an e-mail right back to the hotel," Grandma said. "And you can tell them about your date tonight. They'll be pleased that you're going out and having fun."

"It's not really a date, you know," I told her. "It's just that Collin's being polite. He got those two tickets from his dad, and he's treating your granddaughter."

Grandma snorted. "Not on your Nellie. Being polite has nothing to do with it. I've seen him making goo-goo eyes at you."

I shook my head. "Grandma! You've been reading too many romances."

I wasn't sure I even wanted to go tonight, but I didn't know how to get out of it. What would tomorrow bring? Not only would I know if Kirsty forgave me, but I'd see whatever it was that Miss Lovelace was taking from her safety deposit box for me. How could I play-act at having a good time tonight?

"Like to go to *The Nutcracker* in my place?" I asked Grandma, trying to make it sound like a joke. "Collin's the blond hunk type you've been longing for, in person."

Grandma gave me a swat with the newspaper. "We know he'd love that. Go get yourself ready, girl."

When I came back downstairs, she was sitting on the couch, doing the crossword and listening to a Beatles CD. On the couch beside her was a long white coat of the softest-looking wool.

"This is for you to wear tonight. I don't want you sitting on the North Pole at intermission."

I gasped. "Are you sure I can borrow it? It's so beautiful."

"Try it on, love."

I did. It was perfect.

"Turn the collar up," Grandma advised. "A turned-up white collar is very flattering. It frames the face."

Paul McCartney was singing about his troubles seeming far away. Not mine, I thought. They've been hanging around for quite a long time.

I kept the coat on, the collar up, and sat beside Grandma. The coat was as soft as a cloud. I remembered today in St. Matthew's, the way Noah had given me the blue knitted blanket and told me about talking to Kirsty. There was such an unreality to it, sitting here, the Beatles singing to us, Grandma now and then humming along. Did I actually believe I could talk to someone who was dead? My mind skimmed the surface, not wanting to look at any thought too closely. Kirsty then, crumpled on the grass, blood running out of her mouth, trickling from her ears. Kirsty now . . . where?

I squeezed myself into the corner of the couch.

"Catherine?" Grandma's voice was sharp. "What are you thinking about, child? I can see from your face it's nothing good."

I managed a smile. "This and that. Nothing important."

Grandma leaned close to me. "Why don't you call

one of your friends back home? Gossipy girl talk always helps."

"I don't have any friends back home," I said. "I stopped talking, wouldn't tell them about how it was. . . ." I swallowed a sob. "I couldn't. After a while, they shut me out. I didn't care. I wanted to be by myself anyway."

"Nonsense." Grandma took off her glasses and set them on the end table as if she could inspect me better without them. "You can have your friends back, sweetheart. Friends don't stop being friends because something bad happens to you in your life. I think maybe *you* shut *them* out."

I shrugged. Someone had started a memorial for Kirsty. Everyone had come to love her, her humor, her funny ways. They'd left flowers and notes and candles and a tiny Scottish flag at the spot where my father's Taurus, the car we'd borrowed for the party, careered over the edge. I was still in the hospital, and I was glad. Knowing what I knew, I couldn't have faced it.

My parents drove me out there late one night, when I was sure I wouldn't meet anyone. I left the little kiltie doll I'd brought back from Scotland. I'd bought it in Paisley at the street fair. I scattered flowers at the crash site, and cried, and came home, alive, while Kirsty was dead. Her body had been flown back to Scotland. . . . But I was going to talk with her tomorrow, here, in California. How could she be buried in Kilbarcin and talking to me in Pasadena?

Grandma put her arm around me and pulled me close. "My poor little Catherine," she whispered. "Poor little girl." I felt her cheek, soft as a flower, and smelled her sandalwood perfume.

"I'm OK," I said shakily. "And I know I'm going to be better soon. Tomorrow. When I'm forgiven."

Grandma pulled away a little and looked down at me. "What are you talking about, Catherine?" Then her face brightened. "I bet I know. You're going to talk with Dr. Miller. That would be wonderful. He is so wise and good. You've made an appointment with him for tomorrow?"

"I might see him," I said truthfully.

"I'm glad." We smiled at one another as the doorbell rang. "That sounds like it might be his son, come to call," Grandma said.

And when I opened the door, there he was, wearing dark pants and a leather school jacket, his blond hair sticking up just a little bit in back.

"Hi," we both said at the same time.

"You look nice," he told me.

"You, too."

He smiled and called past me to Grandma, "Hi, Mrs. Larrimer."

"Take good care, both of you," Grandma said. "And whatever you do, have fun."

I promised myself I'd try.

The Pasadena Civic was just a few blocks from Grandma's, but Collin brought his truck. As we came close, I saw that the sidewalks were jammed with people, walking, dressed in winter finery, though it wasn't even chilly by Chicago standards. There was celebration in the air.

I glanced sideways at Collin. He wasn't handsome at all, tall and skinny and long-legged. But there was an easiness about him, a confidence. His whole face seemed to crinkle when he smiled. He had nice, small ears. I hoped I wasn't making goo-goo eyes.

Maybe he caught me looking, because he suddenly said, "I bet you were a really cute little kid. I bet you had those long kind of bangs that came right down to your nose." He gave me that infectious grin. That made me grin back.

"I don't think I even had bangs," I told him. "And I was fat."

"Cute, anyway," he said.

I decided it might not be that hard to concentrate on *The Nutcracker* and Collin Miller tonight.

The Civic Auditorium was a big square building sitting like a mausoleum at the top of wide, shallow steps. A scarlet banner was looped above the doors. THE NUTCRACKER, it proclaimed in large gold letters. I was glad we hadn't had to pass St. Matthew's to get there.

Our tickets came with preferred parking that was in a lot half a block away. We walked back together along the busy sidewalk. People, mostly kids, called out Collin's name as we went up the steps. He waved and called back. I sensed the curious looks at me. Who was this girl with Collin Miller? Hadn't seen her around before. Sometimes Collin pointed at me and called, "This is Catherine," in a braggy kind of voice that seemed to say, "See how lucky I am!"

Our seats were perfect, up in the front balcony. I read the program, leafed through the pages, and told myself to make conversation so I wouldn't be a drag.

"Do you have to train a lot for water polo?" I asked in my best, interested voice.

"Yep. I was in the pool all afternoon."

"Brr," I said.

He grinned. "Not too bad."

"I expect being tall, like you are, must make it easier to score goals," I said, searching desperately for something to talk about.

"Yeah. Sometimes I wonder why I'm not a star. Especially with these big feet of mine." He held one up. "They're like built-in flippers."

I laughed. "They *are* pretty enormous. But if they were small, you'd probably tip over."

It was good sitting in the half-dark, saying ordinary things to someone as nice as Collin.

"Here we go," he whispered as the lights dimmed, the red curtains slid smoothly open, and the dancers came on stage.

I'd seen *The Nutcracker* performed many times, but it's the one ballet that means Christmas to me. I was once one of the sugarplum fairies in our fourth-grade production. I knew the music. I knew the dances and the jokes and exactly what was coming next, but I've always loved it. I let the music and the good memories wash over me, and I was glad I was there, not back at Grandma's, waiting for tomorrow to come.

When Collin asked me at intermission to go out on the patio with him, I said, "It's probably as cold out there as at the North Pole," and smiled when he looked puzzled. So I told him about Grandma and her beau and discovered I was almost enjoying myself.

We talked as we stood outside, sipping mugs of

eggnog. The stars were as sharp as glass in the night sky, and the cheery spill of conversation around me lifted my spirits.

"So you're going home the day after Christmas," Collin said, and when I nodded, he added, "Too bad." I knew he meant it. He liked me. I liked him, too. I wished he lived in Chicago, that I'd met him there and could get to know him better. I wondered if he'd kiss me good night later, and I let my mind enjoy that possibility.

I looked across the patio then and saw two women, standing together, sipping steaming cups of coffee. One of them was Donna Cuesta's mother. She wasn't looking in my direction, and I was glad. My only conversation with her had been so sad and left me feeling helpless and confused. Was she the one who'd told me about the ring Donna wore? Or had that been Grandma? I remembered the "Missing" card with Donna's picture, CALL 1-800-THE-LOST, and although it wasn't that cold, I shivered inside Grandma's soft white coat.

The two women set down their coffee cups and went up the steps. I thought they were going inside, but then I saw Mrs. Cuesta stop by the door, take a bundle of leaflets from her big purse, share some with her friend, and begin handing them out. I knew they had to be about her daughter, and I looked at her anxious, desperate face and felt my heart ache for her. I went in by the door where the friend stood, which took less courage.

"Thanks," I said as I accepted the leaflet and kept on walking. I stared down at it. HAVE YOU SEEN THIS GIRL? was printed across the top in heavy black letters. Underneath, but larger, was the same picture of Donna Cuesta that had been on the 1-800-THE-LOST card and a phone number that was probably her mother's.

It was Collin who said, "She looks kind of like you. Really pretty."

I nodded. "I was thinking the same thing. I mean, not the pretty part. Just the same type." Those words were getting to be so familiar.

I folded the paper small and slid it into the pocket of Grandma's coat. Donna Cuesta, I thought, where are you?

"Poor Mrs. Cuesta," I said. "Did you know her daughter?"

"A little. She was in the youth group at church for a while. After . . . well . . . after her friend's death, she quit coming."

"Her friend's death?" Something frightening here. "What happened?"

I could tell Collin didn't want to talk about it. He stood,

looking down at his feet, scuffing a toe along the cement. "I'm sorry," he said. "I shouldn't be getting into this."

But . . . a friend's death.

"Please tell me," I said. Whatever this was, I felt a quick rush of sympathy for Donna. I knew how it felt to lose a friend. And how odd that she and I, who looked a little alike, had had a similar experience.

"Well." He glanced at me. "There were drugs involved. The paramedics got to Donna in time. They were too late for her friend. After that, Donna went kind of psychotic." He stopped. "You don't want to hear about this, Catherine."

"But I do," I said.

"The rumor was that Donna had supplied the drugs, so you can see why she felt so guilty."

I nodded.

"Then she met some guy, and he helped her a lot. He was good to her, she said."

The bell was ringing for the end of intermission, and people were moving in laughing, talking groups toward the entrance.

I put my hand on Collin's arm. "Wait a sec. Who was this guy? Was his name Noah? Was Noah the one who gave her the ring?"

Collin had started walking toward the auditorium,

quite quickly. I could tell he didn't want to go on with this conversation, but I had to know. "I have no idea what the guy's name was," he said. "And I never noticed any ring."

"Did you talk with Donna at all? I mean, after she met this—this person?"

Collin shook his head. "Ryan Murphy talked to her the day before she disappeared. She told him she was happy now, that everything had been cleared up." He glanced down at me. "Ryan told her mother what she'd said. He told her Donna probably just took off with the guy, which is bad enough, I guess, but could be worse."

I walked beside him, looking up into his face, already knowing in my heart what must have happened.

Oh, Noah! You helped Donna. I don't think she went off with you, because you're still here. But you gave her peace and courage and helped her get past her shame and guilt. You cleared everything up for her. Will you do that for me? Or am I believing just because I want to believe? No. It's possible. Really possible. I was so filled with hope and excitement that I felt like skipping and dancing like a child. Without meaning to, I clapped my hands.

Collin laughed. "You *are* getting into the Christmas spirit."

I smiled up at him. Should I try to tell Mrs. Cuesta that I thought Donna was probably OK? It would help her so much. But how could I explain my thinking? I needed time to come up with a way to do this.

We were back in our seats. The orchestra was playing, the curtains sliding soundlessly open. The auditorium filled with applause.

"Here come the mice again," Collin whispered to me, and he took my hand as if he thought the giant mouse king would freak me out. And when the mice went offstage, he kept my hand warm and safe in his, and I was happy.

Later, he kissed me good night, standing under the Christmas lights on Grandma's porch.

"I had a good time," I told him shakily.

"Me, too. I'm wondering if I could tag you for tomorrow night." He turned down my coat collar in an absentminded way. I left it like that even though my face probably didn't look as nice without its frame.

"I know it's kind of pushy, and I know your grandma probably wants to have you to herself for some of the time you're here, without me horning in. It's just . . . "

"It's just?" I prompted.

"Well, I've only got four more days to . . . " He stopped again and then said, with that nice grin, "four more days to make an impression."

"I'm impressed," I said. "But about tomorrow night—I'll have to see first if Grandma has anything planned." And I thought, by tomorrow night, I might even have more of that Christmas spirit.

"I should let you go in." He held on to my hand. "Can I call tomorrow?"

I nodded. "That would be great. Good night, Collin. Thanks for tonight."

Grandma was playing Solitaire on her laptop when I came in. "You look like a happy girl," she said, glancing up and smiling. "I'll stop this in just a minute. I'm almost finished—darn!" She placed the king of hearts up in a space in the back row. "Did you know," she asked absently, "that each king in a deck of playing cards represents a great king from history?"

"I didn't," I said.

"Well, it's true. As you are aware"—she gave me a roguish glance—"I'm quite a student of history, what with all my scholarly reading. I learned this in *The Young Earl of Stratcommon*. Now, the king of hearts here is

Charlemagne. The king of diamonds is Julius Caesar, spades is King David, and clubs is Alexander the Great."

"You are remarkable," I said.

Grandma nodded. "I am. Now, look over there on the table. An e-mail came for you, and I printed it out. It came to my address, of course, and it's from St. Matthew's, so I'm afraid I read it."

My heart began to beat uncomfortably fast as I walked across to the table. There it was. "I got your message," it said. "I'll see you tomorrow at three."

There was no signature. There didn't have to be.

"I'm guessing it's from Dr. Miller," Grandma said, turning to look at me. "I'm glad you're going to see him, love. You will be helped."

"I know I will," I said.

Charlemagne, Julius Caesar, King David, and Alexander the Great watched me impassively from the computer screen.

The Presence looked with satisfaction around his den. It was all ready for Catherine. His books were neatly arranged. His stereo had the tape of Bach's Pastorale, *just waiting to be turned on. He'd stolen the stereo and CD player from the office a few years back. "Someone* broke in again," Manuel had said, and he'd arranged to have the locks changed. The Presence smiled, remembering. He enjoyed his stolen music. He glanced at the poinsettia he'd taken from Maureen's desk and placed on the table that he sat at to write his memoirs. It made him smile again when he thought of Maureen fussing over where her poinsettia had disappeared to when he'd taken it to add to the others at the altar. Now he'd taken it again. Rita's blue comforter was folded on the recliner chair.

He'd sent the e-mail to reassure Catherine and make certain she'd come. He examined the note she'd written one more time, then placed it carefully in the drawer of his desk. "For afterwards," he told his ladies. The serpent ring with the two red stones was in its velvet box. "You've all worn this," he said, lifting it out. "I've had to take it back from each of you. Not a gentlemanly thing to do, but under the circumstances . . . " There was no light down here, but he had no need of light, and he could see the ring clearly, its red stones glittering, the serpent coiled, at rest.

Soon she'd be here.

He'd try not to frighten her too much. If circumstances had been different, he would have wooed her with *prettier flowers and candy in a red heart-shaped box. They would have kissed and held hands. But those delights had been taken from him. It couldn't be helped. And in time she would love him in spite of what he was. She would love him.*

TEN

*W*hen I woke up next morning, a jumble of thoughts pounded through my mind. Noah today. Miss Lovelace today. I wrapped my arms tight around myself and squeezed my eyes shut. Terrifying, both of these appointments, but necessary, and, in the end, I hoped, good. Fleetingly, I remembered last night and being with Collin. There was a sweetness then. But Collin would have to be on hold till today was over.

"All well this morning?" Grandma asked when I came downstairs.

"Fine." I bent to kiss her cheek, and she laid down the *Times* and smiled up at me.

"Breakfast?" She poured orange juice and passed the toast and coffee.

"Now," she said. "Let's talk about this morning. Since tomorrow is Christmas Eve, I don't have to go in to St. Matthew's. The office is closed till after the holidays and everything's ready for the midnight service. . . ." She paused. "I know you're busy this afternoon."

I pretended to be interested in spreading marmalade on my wheat toast. Busy this afternoon. Busy!

"So," she went on, "I thought we'd go this morning and check out Old Town. It will be fun. The shops are decorated for Christmas, and there are lots of things going on. How does that sound?"

"Sounds cool," I said, thinking it sounded better than staying home watching the clock. Miss Lovelace's nurse had said to come after two. Noah had said to come at three.

There was such a tightness in my throat that I couldn't swallow, and when I took a sip of coffee, I choked. "Sorry," I croaked. My eyes streamed.

"Are you all right, pet?" Grandma had risen to pat my back.

"Fine. A crumb went down the wrong way."

We left as soon as we cleared the dishes. Grandma drove her shiny red Volkswagen, a fresh daisy in the flower holder. The big doors of St. Matthew's were shut tight as we passed. Grandma beeped her little horn. "I always like to say hello to the church," she said.

I glanced up at the red stones of the walls set so tidily together. Grandma loved St. Matthew's. So did my mother. I should, too, because this afternoon I might find my salvation in its holy space. But I was wary of it now. Unsure. Tomorrow I would love it.

Old Town teemed with Christmas crowds, swarming along the narrow sidewalks. Fiddlers fiddled, steel drummers drummed, a clown blew up Santa balloons, and Santa himself posed for pictures beside his sleigh.

We wandered and strolled, stopping now and then to watch a performer. I checked and rechecked my watch. I didn't want time to pass quickly, but that's what I did want. My stomach roiled as I smiled and talked and acted out my part.

"I made lunch reservations here," Grandma said, stopping at a restaurant that looked like a gigantic white tent with two large palm trees reaching up through the roof. She lowered her voice. "You know who owns this place? A movie star."

"Really?" I pretended interest.

"Really. And sometimes he puts in an appearance. Take a look around."

There was no movie star to be seen, but there was a really good Chinese chicken salad and papaya iced tea. Grandma caught me sneaking a look at my watch and said softly, "You'll be in lots of time. Don't worry. I'll drop you off at the church on the way home."

"I'd be way too early for Dr. Miller," I said. "If it's OK, I'll go home first, borrow your bike, and ride over."

"Fine." Grandma reached across the table and took my hands. "I'm glad you're going to talk to him. I'm actually relieved."

Tears gathered behind my eyes. She was so caring, so trusting, and here I was, keeping everything from her. But if I told her now, she'd never let me go. "A psychic— getting you in touch with someone who's dead. Absolutely not. I'm responsible." And so on, ending with, "That's all you need to make you crazy again."

And she might be right. I promised myself that when this was over, I'd never deceive her again. I squeezed her hand. "I love you, Grandma."

"I love you, too, Catherine," she said, and then her face brightened. "Look over there! Look fast! Isn't that what's-his-name in person? The movie star?"

I looked. "If it is, he's smaller than I expected," I said, and Grandma sighed and said, "Just like the *Mona Lisa*."

It was twenty minutes to two when we got home.

"I think I'd like to leave a little early," I told her. "Maybe, you know, get in some quiet thinking."

"I understand."

She didn't, of course. I was giving myself more than enough time to ride first to Miss Lovelace's house.

"Take a sweater, love," Grandma advised. "St. Matthew's can be very cold."

I knew.

Upstairs I grabbed a jacket and tied the sleeves around my waist. In the mirror, I saw me, looking back at myself. White face, black hair, frightened eyes. But soon it would be over. I'd say what I had to say to Kirsty.

And what would that be?

I bit my lips, still staring at myself in the mirror. I'd say, "I know you didn't want to drive. You didn't want to die. Every day I hear your voice, 'You can't do this to me, wee hen. I'm still no' used to the way you Yanks drive on the wrong side of the road. It makes me gey nervous even thinking about it.'"

Her words had come to me that night through a haze of beer, beer that I wasn't used to. Two cans. Two rotten cans. "You'll do it, Kirsty. No problem." My words probably slurred, stupid, thick. Kirsty driving around the bend in the highway, me half-asleep beside her. The Taurus veering to the wrong side of the road. The big truck coming right at us, horn blaring, brakes screeching. Kirsty's scream, the rush of air as the truck passed us, the car wavering, crashing nose first over the embankment, smashing, sliding, coming to a stop. I remember whispering Kirsty's name. I remember—or thought I remembered—her groans. Her pleas for help. That much and then only darkness.

It was a long time before they found us and helicoptered us out. I had a concussion, two broken legs, a crushed pelvis, and eight broken ribs. I never knew a person had that many ribs. Kirsty was dead, her neck broken.

"She died on impact," the police said, as if that made it somehow better. Maybe it did. But, then, how was it she'd spoken? How did they know that for sure?

My fault, every bit of it. And I'd never had the chance to beg her forgiveness. Would I have that chance today? Would she listen? Would she forgive?

I went shakily downstairs.

Grandma came with me to the garage and handed me her helmet. "Here, sweetie, we don't want an accident." She stopped and stared at me, wide-eyed. "Oh, mercy, do I always have to say the wrong thing?"

"You don't, of course. You say what's in your heart, and that isn't wrong."

She held the bike for me to climb on as if I were a little kid. "Take care, Catherine," she said softly, and I nodded, not even able to speak.

I rode fast to Miss Lovelace's, so fast that I was early. When I came to the little park by her house, I wheeled in, propped my bike, and sat on a green-painted seat. Ten minutes to wait.

A little boy and his dad were playing Frisbee on the grass. Pigeons flocked around my feet, then sauntered away, disappointed that I had no food to give them.

I felt the droop of the locket that hung on its little gold chain inside my T-shirt and pulled it up. Inside, facing each other, were two photos, one of me and one of Kirsty. We'd taken the pictures in one of those silly photo booths at the Paisley fair. It was the same day I'd bought the kiltie doll. We'd mugged for the camera, making ridiculous faces, and when we'd gotten back to Kirsty's house, I'd cut the pictures and fitted them into my locket. Kirsty'd said, "You realize when this is closed, we'll be kissing," and we'd staggered around, pretending to throw up.

My hands shook as I clicked the locket shut again and let it hang outside my T-shirt, where it could be seen. Would she see it today? Would she recognize it? Would it make her think of all the good times we'd had, all the closeness?. . . But how could she see or hear or remember? She was dead.

Panic filled me. I couldn't wait another minute. I'd get

whatever Miss Lovelace had for me and go. I wheeled my bike up to her front door and pressed the bell.

The nurse came in what seemed like the same second. "Here." She handed me an ancient-looking brown package maybe six inches by eight, tied with old string. It had *Charlotte Lovelace* written across the front in girlish writing. Underneath, in solid black print, it said, NOT TO BE OPENED UNTIL HER DEATH.

I looked at the nurse. "But . . ."

"You're to open it now," she said. "No one else is to see it." She kept jiggling the door impatiently, as if she had better things to do. "I'm to get your word on that."

Behind her, I could see the picture of Miss Lovelace, so very like me. "You have my word."

"And she wants it back as quickly as you can. It's not to be left for other eyes to see."

I turned the package in my hand. "Thanks. You have my word on that, too."

I felt the nurse watching me as I walked to my bike. I pushed the bike along beside me, holding the package in my free hand. It was bulky but not heavy. There were different thicknesses inside, something square and hard.

I glanced at my watch. Almost an hour to wait. Noah probably wouldn't be there yet. I wanted to rush, to hurry to get there, but the church doors wouldn't even be open till he came.

The boy and his dad were still playing Frisbee in the park. A gardener was snipping dead heads off the pink camellias that bordered the path. I made myself sit in the same seat and ease the string off the envelope. NOT TO BE OPENED UNTIL HER DEATH. The words made me crawly inside. Kirsty was dead.

I spread my jacket across my knees and lifted everything out. There was a small notebook with a worn leather cover, the gold letters DIARY 1928 almost rubbed away. There was a bundle of letters tied with a bedraggled blue ribbon, a folded yellowed piece of newspaper, and a photograph.

I picked the photograph up. Written on the back was the name Noah. When I turned it over, it was totally blank. The image that must have been of Noah's grandfather had faded to nothingness, the picture lost somewhere in time. I glanced again at my watch, opened the diary, and began to read.

Usually the Presence didn't bother about time. Why should he, when he had all the time in the world? But sometimes, like today, he was impatient, and he'd go check the office clock. Almost an hour till she'd be here.

He wandered into the library. The Presence knew that he'd been deprived when he was young. His "parents" had never read to him. He'd never had his own children's books, not even one. Sometimes he told himself grimly that he'd come to fairy tales and fantasy and Mother Goose too late in life. . . . Still, he loved them now. He had his favorites. The Little Prince, The Phantom Tollbooth, and, of course, The Secret Garden. Oh, to have friends like Mistress Mary and Dickon, to have a garden of his own and a bird to sing to him.

He shook his head. Stop it, Noah. Soon you will have your heart's desire. You will have Catherine.

Some poems he knew by heart, like that one by William Allingham. He sat in Maureen's swivel chair and said softly,

> "Four ducks on a pond,
>   A grass-bank beyond,
>   A blue sky of spring,
>   White clouds on the wing;
>   What a little thing
>   To remember for years—
>   To remember with tears!"

He had no sweet place like that to remember, even with tears.

He whirled himself faster and faster in the chair.

"It is good to be merry and wise," he told the old calendar on the wall, the one with the black dog and the white kitten playing together.

> "It is good to be merry and wise.
> It is good to be honest and true.
> It is best to be off with the old love
> before you are on with the new."

Once, he hadn't followed that advice, and it had almost ended in disaster. But now he would have Catherine. He would have another chance.

He thought about how he would treat her. How he'd share his books and music and the feelings he had inside of him. With Catherine, everything would be perfect.

E L E V E N

*J*une 3, the diary began. No year. Then a sentence in block letters.

TODAY I MET HIM. *His name is Noah Vanderhorst, and, of all places, I met him in St. Matthew's. He's 17, same as me. And so handsome I could swoon. He's mysterious, too, and exciting, so exciting. He goes to art school, and he says Reverend Maxwell allows him to use a little apartment downstairs in the church. That way, he can save on rent. An impoverished artist, not in an attic but a basement. How romantic. Maybe he'll let me see his rooms when I know him better.*

How strange this was, reading the words of the girl who was the same age then as I am now. Today she was old and frail. Why did she want me to read her diary? Why was she so frantic that I should read all this about my Noah's grandfather?

My Noah! What was I thinking?

I came to the church this afternoon to meet him. Mother had flowers to deliver to decorate the altar for tomorrow's service. She was pleased when I said I would take them. Ooh-la-la! Lottie taking such a sudden interest in the church! I only hope and pray that Noah doesn't find out about me. But how could he? I won't let myself spoil this by worrying.

I looked up from the pages. A mother pushed a stroller along the path and smiled at me as she passed. She and the baby were both wearing Christmas red.

I was wondering what secret Lottie had that she didn't want Noah to discover. And I was thinking how many strange coincidences there were. I looked like Lottie. I'd met her Noah's grandson, and I had a secret, too. Of course, Kirsty had told him mine. And then there was poor Donna Cuesta and the ring and more coincidences.

I checked my watch. Twenty minutes to three. I had time to read on.

June 15

I know I'm in love. Noah and I have been meeting every chance I get. He is always there in the church, and he is so mysterious about what he does there. On Tuesdays and

Thursdays, Mother goes to her bridge afternoons and social club. I go to Noah. He hasn't invited me to his rooms. I would love it if he did. If that is shameful, I don't care. It excites me the way he looks at me. There is such passion in his eyes. Did I mention that his eyes are big and dark and deep? Inscrutable. Sometimes I think there is no light in them at all. He looks like Rudolf Valentino. He strokes my hair and I tingle. I have not felt so alive since before I did that awful thing to the baby.

I had to stop reading. A tree filled with tiny golden leaves rustled behind my bench. The leaves sighed and whispered, shocked as I was at the words in the diary. I could hear my heart pounding. She had done some awful thing. And me? I had done an awful thing, too.

Did I mention that Noah has the coldest hands? Poor Noah! I know they embarrass him. Sometimes he wears gloves. "Cold hands, warm heart," he says.

Something really strange here. Those cold hands. Were there just too many coincidences? And if they weren't coincidences, then what were they? Of course, the coldness could be genetic, passed down from grandfather to son to grandson.

I began flipping pages, needing to find out more, quickly. Here and there I'd pick up a phrase.

I asked if we could meet somewhere else, not in the church, but he said no. It's private there. He shouldn't be seen with a member of the congregation. The Reverend might ask him to give up his apartment, and he couldn't afford that.

I flipped again.

He hasn't kissed me yet. I've been forward enough to suggest it, not in words, but by the way I lean toward him. It has been embarrassing when he moves away. But I admire him. It would be so easy to take advantage of me here in the privacy of the church. And he has given me the ring that was his grandmother's. This must be significant.

I turned more pages, then stopped abruptly on July 2—stopped because the first two words were in heavy black letters and underlined.

<u>He knows</u>. *But how does he know? Nobody does except Reverend Maxwell, who counseled me and who promised me that my confession was between a minister and one of his flock, sacred and secret unto death. So how does he know?*

He held my hands, his thick in those gray woolen gloves. And looked at me with such compassion. "I believe you didn't mean to hurt the baby," *he said.* "It was an unfortunate accident."

My heart just about stopped beating. I thought it better to tell him the truth, if we are going to move forward with our relationship. "The baby was crying so hard," *I said.* "My aunt Cissie had told me to give her a bottle of water and sugar, but she kept spitting it out and crying and crying and crying. I had one of my headaches."

Noah kept murmuring things like, "Poor Lottie. Poor little Lottie."

I told him how I shook her. "I didn't mean to be rough. I didn't think I was—"

"Shh, sweetheart." *He whispered those words so close to my ear that I could feel his breath, so cold. Why is he always so cold?*

"The baby went into a spasm and then she lay still, and I didn't know what to do, so I left her in the crib, and when my mother and Aunt Cissie came home, I told them she was sleeping, and I never, never . . . "

"It's all right, little one," he said, and I felt sure then that he'd take me in his arms and I could cry and he'd comfort me, but all he did was pat my shoulder. And then he said the strangest thing. "Death isn't the worst thing that can happen, you know. Death and forgetting and peace. I recommend it."

That startled me so much. I thought I hadn't understood him. He couldn't mean that death was good? And recommending it, as if he knew?

The diary shook in my hands. Shivers trembled across my skin. She'd killed a baby! A baby! My God, a baby!

I put on my jacket, which I'd left on the bench beside me. The pigeons I'd seen earlier had come back around my feet. They were pecking through the fallen golden leaves, stopping now and then to crane their shimmery necks and stare at me.

There was such a horrible familiarity to Lottie's story, as if I'd heard it before or lived it myself. We'd both killed someone.

Stop it, Catherine. Just stop it.

It was five minutes to three. I needed to go, but the urge to keep reading was so compelling that I couldn't. I decided two more pages, that was all.

He says he can let me talk to Baby Joan. "What?" I asked. "How can I talk to a baby? A dead baby."

"That was four years ago," he said. "She's a little girl now and wise. Do you think time stops when you're dead?"

I couldn't believe what I was hearing.

"I have this gift," he said. "I'm able to reach those who have passed on. You can speak with little Joan and tell her how sorry you are. She'll forgive you. Death is not that bad. Believe me, Joanie is happy, and she carries no grudge."

"You've talked with her already?" I asked.

"Yes," he said.

I know I must have looked as frozen as I felt.

"Are you a psychic?" I asked.

"Not a psychic. I just have this God-given ability."

I slammed the diary shut and stood up. No more! No more! I could hardly breathe. The same questions I had asked, the same answers. I stood, holding the diary against my chest, then slid it back into the envelope. What was going on?

My legs were so weak, I had trouble cycling back to Grandma's. No way could I go to the church and face Noah. My thoughts tumbled round in a crazy circle. Warned! Warned! But I couldn't get myself to believe that *this* Noah and *that* Noah were the same person. That would be totally insane. Lottie's Noah had been young way back in time. What was I letting myself imagine?

I parked the bike in the garage, ran in and up the stairs. I slid the package carefully under my pillow, then took it out and put it in a drawer. Too close under my pillow. Too personal. Later I'd have to lay my head there and sleep and dream.

Grandma was baking cookies. The kitchen was a mess. There were bowls and scrapers and mixers and open bags of this and that. Chocolate chips had spilled on the counter.

"Why am I doing this?" she asked me in a distracted way. "I think it must be a grandma thing, and I don't get to be a grandma up close all that often. Anyway, they smell good, don't they? I won't guarantee how they'll taste."

"They'll taste good, too," I murmured. The smell was making me sick because I was sick already.

"You're back early, child," she said.

I nodded.

"Was it helpful?"

I nodded again, not trusting myself to speak.

Grandma scraped cookie dough off her fingers and into the garbage disposal. She looked over her shoulder at me as she washed her hands. "What's wrong, Catherine?"

Her soft, caring voice was too much, and I began to sob.

"Sweetie! Sweetie." Her arms were tight around me. "I expect it was hard, talking about everything to Dr. Miller, living it all again. But it will be easier now. I know it will."

I clung to her as if she was my last sane hope in an insane world.

She patted my back, her still-wet hands damp through my light jacket. "I know something to cheer you up." She held me away from her and smiled. "Collin called. He wanted to know if he could see you tonight. And then, nice boy that he is, he asked if I could spare you since your time is so short. And selfish old lady that I am,

I told him I saw no reason why he and I shouldn't share you." She fished a tissue out of the pocket of her jeans and gave it to me. "So he's coming for dinner."

She yawned an exaggerated yawn. "Since I didn't get my reading nap today, and now that I've done all this cooking or baking or whatever you call it, I expect I'll go to bed early and leave you two youngsters to your own devices."

"Oh, Grandma!" I gave a choked-up laugh. "I hope you didn't tell him that!"

"Of course I did. Why do you think he's so eager to come?"

The doorbell rang. "Who?" Grandma began, and I thought, "Could it be Noah?" Had he come to find out why I hadn't gone to St. Matthew's? Why did the thought of Noah terrify me now? Because . . . because . . .

I stood, not wanting to go into the living room and open the door. Grandma moved quickly past me.

"My goodness," I heard her say in a happy voice. "What a lovely surprise!"

She spoke over her shoulder to me. "It's Maureen and Rita and Arthur, come to call. And bearing gifts."

Rita laughed. "Sorry, Eunice. They're for Catherine, not for you."

"Well, I'm definitely sorry, too," Grandma said. "But come in. We have chocolate-chip cookies."

She was so normal. Everything was so normal and so unreal.

I let out a deep breath. Had I really thought it might be Noah? He wouldn't want to come visit Grandma. How did I know that? I just did.

Our three visitors were filled with Christmas cheer. They smiled at me, asked how I was enjoying my stay, and each presented me with a small gift-wrapped package.

Grandma admired Maureen's green fingernails with holly berries painted on them. "Very festive," she said.

I touched Arthur's hand. "This is so nice of you. I haven't seen you for a couple of days." That was when I'd gone up the stairs to the gallery to check if there was someone there because I'd heard a voice—Noah's voice. Where had Noah hidden himself that day?

I stood, holding the three little packages, trying hard not to let my mind jump again to those awful suspicions. "Shall I open them now?" I asked.

"Do," Rita urged. "It's more fun for us."

They beamed with anticipation as I unwrapped.

There was a pretty chain with garnets spaced around it, from Maureen. "This is so pretty," I told her.

"The stones aren't real," she said. "But it's quite tasteful. I would have liked to have gotten you something more showy, but Rita said I'd better not."

That made me smile for real.

"This is perfect," I said.

From Rita, I got matching garnet earrings, and from Arthur, a sparkling butterfly clip to hold back my hair.

"I thought it would be jolly for the holidays," he said shyly, and I lifted two wings of my hair and clipped them back. "Lovely," he said.

I managed to hug all three of them at once.

"How am I going to go home and leave you guys?" I asked and added, "Wait, I have something for you."

I'd brought hologram cards with me from the Field Museum to give as small gifts if I needed them. They showed Sue the dinosaur. When you moved the card, Sue's neck of bones stretched toward you.

The cards were on top of the dresser. In the drawer below was the diary. I had to look at it again. It couldn't, *couldn't* be as bad as I thought. I slid the drawer open.

Downstairs I could hear the cheerful voices and Maureen's ready laugh.

The diary.

With one finger, I flipped over a page.

How can I believe what he is saying about himself? That he is immortal? That he has been alive, or dead and alive again, for more than a century? That he is a ghost? But what else can explain all that is mysterious and, yes, frightening about him?

"No," I whispered. "No." I felt so dizzy I had to hold onto the edge of the dresser. With my elbow, I pushed the drawer closed. "Alive, or dead and alive again." A ghost. It couldn't be. This girl, this Lottie was crazy. It was her craziness that was terrifying me, the nonsense she'd written.

But although I was telling myself it was nonsense, I was remembering the way he appeared and disappeared, the way this Noah could talk to those who had "passed over," the way he knew so many secrets.

I went slowly downstairs, holding tight to the banister.

Maureen and Rita and Arthur oohed and aahed over the cards. I told them that yes, I'd seen Sue in person, and yes, she was just as big and ferocious as they imagined. I was having trouble speaking. My mouth felt full of cotton.

"If you smell burning, don't worry," Grandma told me cheerfully. "The first batch of cookies was fine. The second, we can scrape."

She made tea, and I helped her set out her pretty china cups and fill a plate from the first batch, and we sat eating and drinking, talking happy holiday talk. I nodded and smiled and hoped I looked sane, while the lights on Grandma's little tree blinked white and the poinsettias by the window glowed with their red Christmas glow.

"Did you like the flowers I gave you?" he'd asked. Noah! Noah the ghost?

Upstairs, waiting for me, waiting for the night, was the diary. Nothing in the world seemed real.

Our guests left at five-thirty, complimenting Grandma on her cookies and her oolong tea. We stood in the doorway to wave goodbye.

When the phone in the kitchen rang, Grandma picked it up. "Hello," she said. "Hello." Quickly she smashed the receiver down, scowling at it. "That's the third 'nobody there' call since this afternoon," she said. "What's the matter with these people?"

I knew it was Noah. He was wondering why I hadn't come. He was going to tell me how disappointed Kirsty was. Oh, Kirsty, what am I going to do? I'm scared to death of Noah now. But what if he can put me in touch with you? If there's a chance, I have to try. Wait for me, Kirsty. I won't walk away from you again.

The Presence sat in the church office, hunched over in Rita's chair. Only three days till Catherine went home. No time to waste. What had happened today? Her grandmother made plans and she couldn't get away? Or had something alerted her? He couldn't think what it might be.

He glared at the phone. Three times he'd called, and there'd been only the grandmother. He'd had the awful thought that maybe Catherine had been called back to Chicago unexpectedly, that he'd lost her. What else would keep her from Kirsty?

He tapped a pencil on the desk. She'd come. Almost all of them did in the end. She'd come.

*C*ollin would be here at seven. Invited by Grandma, trying to cheer me. If she only knew how much I wished he wasn't coming. How could I talk to him, be pleasant, eat dinner, behave as if my life and I were both sane?

It was six o'clock. I helped Grandma set the table with her pretty red Christmasy placemats and dark green napkins.

She slid a lasagna out of the refrigerator and peeled off the plastic wrap. "No time for real cooking at Christmas," she said. "But I bought this at Trader Joe's, so it will be good."

"And you have the cookies for dessert." I was proud of myself for remembering that and being with it enough to say it.

When she opened the oven door, the heat blasting at my face made my stomach roil. How was I going to get through tonight?

I told Grandma I needed to change and rushed up to my room, straight to the drawer, to the diary. I couldn't leave it alone. Standing there, I read.

Oh, God! Oh, help me, someone! I am lost. I have to put what happened on paper because there is no person on earth whom I can tell, who would believe me.

The writing was a child's scrawl, up and down the page, lines crooked and running into each other. Fear was in every word.

My chest hurt, and I rubbed at it with my fist.

Yesterday, he said he would take me to his room. But I couldn't go to St. Matthew's because my mother had arranged for both of us to attend a recital in the music room of the Green Hotel. The cellist is a friend of my grandparents'. I couldn't get out of it. And I couldn't get word to Noah.

So today I went to St. Matthew's to look for him. There is a new custodian. He was painting the outside window of the choir room, and he let me in when I said I was troubled and needed to pray. Forgive me, God, because all I wanted was to see Noah.

And I saw him. Oh, yes, I saw him. And then I did pray.

I am writing this at night. Can he come here and get me? Oh, I am so scared. And my guilt and burden is worse than before.

I stopped reading, gripping the edge of the open drawer till my knuckles ached. This was about Lottie, more than eighty years ago, but it was about me, too. I felt it in my blood and bones.

Music, sweet and somehow sad, drifted up from downstairs, and then I heard Grandma singing in a wobbly voice about memories, and how they lit the corners of her mind.

There was a small silence. Then I heard a loud "Drat!" before the singing started again. So ordinary, so everyday normal.

I flipped to the next page of the diary.

I couldn't find him at first. He'd said his apartment was in the basement. I started down the stairs. It was very dark, dark as Hell must be. I called his name, but softly, in case the new custodian had come in and might hear. I felt along the wall, down, down, down. There must be a light switch, but I couldn't find one.

I went back upstairs. It was so silent in the church, so filled with cold. There was a flashlight, a big one, on a table in the office. I took it and went back to the basement stairs. Down and down.

At the bottom of the stairs, I came to a big room

that was almost empty. My beam of light showed me only crumbling walls, boxes and things stored, old pews piled on top of each other, everything coated with dust. There were two armchairs, the stuffing hanging out of them, and on the back wall, a big stone fireplace, blackened with age, adorned with stone carvings. No one here.

I was about to leave when I heard faint voices. Oh, if only I'd gone before I heard what I heard.

The voices came from behind the wall at the back, where the fireplace was. I tiptoed across and put my ear to the old plaster. If there was a door, I couldn't see it. Immediately, I knew that one of the speakers was Noah. The other was a girl.

My heart sank. He had someone in there with him. An ordinary girl, without problems, not like me.

I listened hard. The words were muffled, and I couldn't understand most of them. If only God in His mercy had kept me from understanding any of them.

Lottie's own words ran off the page here. I hardly had the strength to hold the diary closer to the floor lamp and struggle with what was crammed into the margin.

"Let me go," the girl was saying. "You have no use for me anymore." And something else, something about never telling and her honor.

Noah's voice then. "I can't—" Something unintelligible. And then I thought I heard the word "disappointed."

"Are you . . . kill . . . ?"

I'm trying to write this word after word as I remember them, though I don't believe I'll ever forget.

I should have run right then, gotten away, but I didn't. Maybe I was numb with shock.

Noah was talking again, his voice raised, and, God help me, I heard everything. "Why would I kill you? My ladies are precious to me. Belinda, my dear, don't cry. There, there, don't cry."

I breathed again. This girl, this Belinda, was simply being dramatic. Of course he wasn't going to kill her. I thought of the kindness in his voice when he'd talked to me.

There was a silence. I imagined him holding her, comforting her, and I almost felt jealous.

"I admit I have been disappointed," he said. There was that word again. "But why do you think . . . died . . . tried to make you love me . . . gave you . . . "

"I do love you. I do." Her voice was terrified.

My ear ached from being pressed so hard against the fireplace. But I couldn't risk missing a word.

I remembered how he'd told me that death wasn't the worst thing. How strange he'd sounded. My stomach cramped with fear.

"Catherine?" Grandma was calling from the bottom of the stairs.

I dropped the diary back in the drawer and came to my door.

"Could you come down here for a minute, love? My amber beads broke. Some of them rolled under the fridge, and I can't reach them."

"Sure," I called.

Beads under the fridge. A girl prisoner. A ghost who might be going to kill her. The words I'd read, so horrifying. The words Grandma spoke, so ordinary. How could I hold them together in my head without going crazy?

The beads had rolled to a stop way at the back. I could see the gleam and glow of them when I crouched down. Grandma brought me a wire coat hanger, and I lay on my stomach and dragged them out.

"Clever girl," Grandma said.

I ran back upstairs. No time now to read more. I had to hurry. But . . . but I had to read more.

The page was still open where I'd last read.

"You are very pretty and a good companion," he was saying to the poor girl, whoever she was. "But I've met someone else."

Did he mean me?

I thought I heard him move, and that unlocked my muscles and started my blood flowing again. What if he came out and found me here?

I turned and ran behind one of the old, bulky armchairs. I clicked off the flashlight, and dark came down all around me—terrifying, breathless dark.

Then there was a slant of flickering light, a grinding noise, and I saw Noah standing in the big fireplace. The whole center of it was now just space. Somehow it had opened, and I could tell there was a room, a secret room, concealed behind it.

He was half-turned, speaking over his shoulder. I tried to peer past him to whatever— whoever—was in there, but his shape blocked the opening.

"What can I cook for you tonight?" he asked the hidden person. "You must be tired of those beans. I'll see if some-

thing more interesting has been left in the Food for the Poor box. Tonight's supper should be special. Poor little Belinda!" he added. "Poor little girl!"

I heard a wail. It could have been a cat. I knew it wasn't.

Dim light oozed out. I saw him press something at the side, a shadowed bump, maybe one of the carvings, and I heard the grinding noise again, as the fireplace closed behind him.

He was standing not ten yards away from me. I cowered behind the chair, my eyes squeezed shut, praying and praying. I couldn't see him, but I heard his soft footsteps pass me, go up the stairs. Did he have eyes for the dark, like a big stalking cat?

I waited, then felt my way along the wall, not daring to switch on the flashlight. Up the stairs, listening, praying, remembering how he could suddenly seem to appear out of nowhere. What if he appeared now, beside me? In the sanctuary. No sign of him as I ran, ran, ran, ran. . . .

"Catherine?" Grandma's voice again, calling cheerfully from the bottom of the stairs. "Honey, Collin will be here any minute."

I had to lick my lips and swallow against the dryness

in my throat. I had to try twice before my voice came out. "Coming," I croaked.

I slammed the diary shut, slammed the drawer to keep it in. What had I read? It couldn't be true. No way. But . . . My mind was a jumble of belief and disbelief.

I pulled off my clothes, grabbed my black velvet pants and a pale blue sweater. I couldn't get the top button on the pants fastened. My fingers belonged to somebody else, somebody uncooperative. My black velvet clogs were somewhere under the bed, and I had to kneel to find them.

I had to lean my head on the comforter while I said over and over, "Not true, not real, not true, not real."

My face, pale and haunted, stared back at me from the mirror as I brushed my hair. The doorbell was ringing.

"All right," I told my reflection. "You are going to be reasonable tonight. You are not going to scare Grandma. Do you want to be rushed off to talk with a shrink again? Do you want to go back into the hospital?"

I went downstairs.

T H I R T E E N

*C*ollin sat on the couch, and Grandma was in the low dark blue chair. When he saw me, Collin stood and handed me a long-stemmed red rose. He looked awkward and embarrassed, as if he didn't do something like this too often. "For you."

"Oh, thanks." I bent to smell the sweetness of its perfume.

"I bring you flowers," Noah had said.

Noah, stay out of my head.

"I love roses," I whispered, and Grandma beamed.

"I had a beau who brought me a dandelion once," she said. "The fluffy kind, you know, that you blow on and make a wish. And right there and then, in my mother's hallway, he blew on it, and seeds just flew everywhere." She waved her arms like windmills. "'I wish that you would be my sweetheart forever and ever,' he said, and I said, 'I wish you'd just clean up the mess you've made before my mother sees it,' and I went and got him a broom and dustpan. He didn't do a very good job. All spring, I kept waiting for dandelions to sprout between the tiles in our hallway."

"You weren't very romantic, Mrs. Larrimer," Collin said, grinning.

"Ah, but I am now," Grandma said. "The older I get, the more romantic I become. It's very pleasant."

"She's OK, your grandma," Collin said as she left to get a vase.

He and I sat side by side on the couch. I tried to make myself think only of now and being here and to keep bad thoughts out of my head.

"Did you have a good day?" Collin asked, and I knew that he wasn't comfortable, either. Maybe I was giving off some kind of anxiety vibes.

"Real good," I lied, wishing Grandma would hurry back.

She brought a slim crystal flute, and I put the rose in it and set it on the table. "Pretty," I told Collin.

He said the Trader Joe lasagna was great.

I could only eat a little.

"She's not dieting," Grandma told him. "It's just she eats like a sparrow."

I tried to laugh. "I've heard sparrows eat a lot. I think they eat their own weight in food every day. Something like that."

"I do, too," Collin said.

Grandma asked him about the water polo team and about what college he wanted to go to and if he thought he'd like to go into the ministry like his father, which made him roll his eyes.

"I've had some offers of scholarships," he said. "I think I might go to the Air Force Academy. I like what they do there."

We talked about how badly we were treating the environment and about global warming and about movies we'd seen and concerts, and I tried hard to act interested. But I wasn't interested, not a bit. I didn't care. This guy's going to think I'm a total washout, I thought. And I didn't care about that, either. There was something I wanted desperately to ask, but I didn't know how.

The phone rang. Grandma answered and snarled into it, "Get a life!"

"Nobody there," she told us. "Again. If it wasn't that your parents might call, Catherine, I'd take the thing off the hook."

Of course it was Noah. Go away, Noah.

We had cookies and ice cream for dessert, and then Grandma said she was going up to bed. There was a choral concert on NPR she wanted to hear and, besides, she was kind of sleepy. And then there was her book.

"I'm at a good, yummy part," she said, smiling broadly. "Informative, too."

"And what does that mean exactly, Mrs. Larrimer?" Collin asked, wide-eyed and innocent.

"I learn a lot," Grandma said, as innocent as he was.

Now, I thought. I'm going to ask now.

"I was wondering," I said, proud of my light, casual voice, "is there ever any talk ghosts haunting the halls of St. Matthew's?"

Grandma's brow wrinkled. "Heavens, child. What a strange question." She stared across at me. "You don't think . . . you don't think you saw something there, Catherine?"

"Oh, Grandma. Don't look so worried." I smiled a reassuring smile. Her worry was over my mental state, of course, not the possibility or the impossibility of a haunted church. "I was just wondering." Oh, gosh, now I was stuttering. "Such an old building—you know. Sometimes . . . "

Collin leaned way back in his chair, stretched his long legs, laced his hands behind his head, and stared at the ceiling. "There *was* the little girl, remember, Mrs. Larrimer."

Grandma frowned. "Oh, that. That was all nonsense, of course. And so long ago. Everyone knows the story just grew and grew, making something out of nothing."

"Tell me," I said.

"Oh, there's nothing really to tell. Just a silly legend. Way before my time, before you or Collin were even born."

"You tell me, Collin." I faked a laugh. "I like ghost stories. Was the little girl . . . a ghost?"

"Catherine!" Grandma stood up. "I don't think this is the kind of thing we should be talking about. Bad dreams all around."

Poor Grandma. I could tell the subject of ghosts was too close to the subject of death, was too close to the subject of Catherine killing her friend. She didn't want old agonies surfacing.

"It's all right, Grandma," I said. "I want to know."

"OK?" Collin asked Grandma, and she gave the slightest of shrugs.

"Let's see how it went." His eyes were fixed again on the ceiling. "Oh, yeah. Her name was Grace Feathertree. She and her parents came to St. Matthew's from South Dakota. They were Native Americans, Ojibwa. Right, Mrs. Larrimer? Right so far?"

"That's the story," Grandma said. "For what it's worth."

The phone rang.

"Not again," Collin said.

It was beside me. I felt I had to be the one to pick it up.

"Catherine?" He didn't need to say who it was. I touched the roundness of my gold locket under my sweater. For courage.

"Why didn't you come today?" he asked. "I waited. Kirsty waited. She says if you don't come tomorrow, she'll close the curtain again. She says she won't wait the way she did when you didn't show up for the Chieftains' concert. She says that time she waited in the rain for two hours."

"She knows what happened," I began and then stopped. I didn't need to tell Noah my good excuse for not turning up that day. Who was I talking to anyway? A ghost who might be a murderer? A ghost who knew secrets, who knew everything?

But how *did* he know about the Chieftains' concert? Was it still possible that he had talked to Kirsty? As a ghost, maybe?

No. He knew things because he listened. He listened

to Grandma telling her friends how I regretted even the littlest ways I'd hurt Kirsty. I spread my guilt around.

"You'd better come tomorrow at three o'clock," he whispered. "Or she'll be gone from you forever and ever."

I bit the inside of my lip and tasted blood, as salty as tears.

"Who was that?" Grandma asked sharply as I slid the phone back in place. She loved me, and she sensed a wrongness.

"It was nobody," I said, stunned at the truth of the words even as I said them. The old, almost forgotten childhood poem flashed into my head:

> As I was going up the stair
> I met a man who wasn't there.
> He wasn't there again today.
> I wish that man would go away.

Noah. The man who wasn't there.

"Collin? Go on about the little girl," I whispered. "I want to hear." I leaned across and covered Grandma's hand with mine. "It won't freak me out. Honest."

"OK," Collin said. "Let me think. I guess she was about five. The story is she was born in some sort of shroud."

"Caul," Grandma said. "Not a shroud, for heaven's sake. A caul is a kind of covering that's around some people when they're born. But it's nonsense to think it gives that person special powers." She looked at me. "Are you sure you want to hear this, Catherine? It's stupid, but it's also a little scary."

"I do want to hear," I said.

Collin looked from me to Grandma. She spread her hands. "Better just finish it now you've started."

"Supposedly, little Grace was in Sunday School, in Oak Chapel, the tiny room at the back of the church. The kids were supervised, but somehow she wandered away and went down the stairs into the basement. No one goes down there anymore. There's no light and no heat and parts of it are sealed off because of insurance and stuff. Maybe it was different then. They started looking for Grace, and she came stumbling up. I guess she'd cut her hands and her knees falling on the steps, and they were all bloody. She looked really weird and then . . . " Collin stopped for effect.

"Go on," I urged.

"When you're telling a good ghost story, you have to wait a few heartbeats at the grisly part." Collin grinned a maniacal grin. "Then Grace spoke. Her voice had totally changed. It was way deep. 'I smell evil and death in the shades below,' she growled. They said her voice sounded like the girl in *The Exorcist*, not like her little baby voice at all. But at least her head didn't turn around backward, like in the movie."

"I'm surprised somebody hasn't made up that little detail," Grandma said. "What a bunch of twaddle. The child probably said she smelled a bad smell. Damp and mildew."

I was stretched tight, icy inside. "*Shades below*," I repeated. "Those don't seem like words a little girl would know."

Grandma snorted. "They seem like an embellishment to me. Somebody making up a story."

"Anyway, her parents left St. Matthew's. Took off for someplace that smelled better." Collin knocked on the table. "And that's all, folks!"

The shades below, where Lottie had been, and Belinda. And where I was invited.

In the shades below, the Presence paced his room, impatient and angry. He'd told her, warned her, that Kirsty wouldn't wait any longer. Was that enough? Would she come?

He made himself sit and read from the book of poetry that he'd taken from the library. Browning, Robert, 1812–89.

Idly, he thought that if he should ever write that autobiography he was planning, there'd be no end date for him. Just Noah Vanderhorst, 1864–?

Those kinds of thoughts usually amused him. Or depressed and frightened him. Forever. More long years, a prisoner in the church. Long years alone.

He opened the book and found the lines that he liked best:

> Whence the grieved and obscure waters slope
> Into a darkness quieted by hope;

Hope to quiet his darkness.
The hope of Catherine.

FOURTEEN

I don't know much about what Collin and I did that
night or what we talked about. I know he found *It's a
Wonderful Life* on television, and we watched it. I smiled
when he smiled, laughed when he laughed, not seeing the
pictures that flickered in front of me. There wasn't much
of the diary left to read. I wished I could just go up to my
room and finish it.

I made hot chocolate for us and brought in some of
Grandma's cookies. I nodded my head and tried to look
interested when Collin talked.

I know my parents called. They were back in London.
It was cold and wet but still bright with the Christmas
spirit. My dad said the people were "off their rockers"
about the rise of gangs and crime. But it seemed peaceful to
him and Mom. He said "off their rockers" was an old ex-
pression he'd latched on to, much used in England. He said
the food was great but different. Steak-and-kidney pud-
ding, meat pies, Scotch eggs. They loved it all.

I guess I made the right sounds and gave the right
answers.

But when Mom came on, she asked, "Are you really all right, Best Girl?" as if she sensed or suspected something was not all right at all.

Tears choked my throat. Mom liked to call me "Best Girl." When I was little, she'd sing a baby song to me:

> "Best Girl in the whole wide world.
> Nobody else will do.
> Best girl that ever was.
> I love you."

I swallowed hard. "Best Girl's OK," I whispered.

"Promise?"

"Promise."

"Just three days and we'll be home, and you'll be home with us." She waited a minute and then said softly, "We'll call again tomorrow night, early. Before your Christmas Eve service."

"Good," I said.

Tomorrow night. How many things will have happened by tomorrow night?

"You miss them?" Collin asked.

I nodded. "It's silly. They'll be back in a few days. And they've only been gone a week. It's just, when I hear their voices and think of them being so far away . . . " I let the words snuffle off.

Collin nodded. "My dad was gone for two months once, building houses in Africa with some other church people. I bawled every time he called home. You just want to be able to touch."

"I know."

He glanced sideways at me. "And I wasn't in first grade at the time, either. That was last year."

I smiled. Nice that he'd admit to something like that. A lot of guys wouldn't.

When I sat back down, he curled an arm casually around my shoulders. It felt so good there, so steady, that I let my head relax into the comfort of it. He was wearing a navy blue sweater, the wool scratchy against my skin. My dad has a sweater like that, scratchy to everyone but him.

Collin's head moved closer to mine. His lips brushed my cheek. I turned my face, and we kissed. It was nice. His mouth was warm and dry and kind.

For a minute, I thought of telling him everything. But then I imagined his startled look, his embarrassment, the fumbling for words, what to say to this crazy girl with her crazy stories. This one was "off her rocker" for sure. She'd been off it before.

Talk about little Grace, who'd been born in a caul! Tell him.

I couldn't.

I let my cheek rub gently against his. I knew we could have liked each other a lot if things had been different.

"Do you think we could do something tomorrow?" he asked. "Maybe drive up to Angeles Crest. There's snow. 'Course, I know snow's nothing new for you, living in Chicago, but still. . . . It's pretty. Sometimes you can see all the way to the ocean. Hard to believe we have snow in California, huh? Or we could pack a picnic lunch and ride our bikes down to Tournament Park. There's a band playing Christmas music tomorrow afternoon."

"I think Grandma has something she wants us to do tomorrow," I said, and I felt bad, lying to him. Except it probably wasn't a lie. I'd have to dodge Grandma's plans, too, if . . .

"We'll be going to the Christmas Eve service tomorrow night," I told him. "So I'll see you there."

Collin beamed. "Absolutely."

At the door, he kissed me again. His kiss was gentle and sweet and unsure. I could tell he was deflated. No response from Best Girl. No holding or clinging. I was sorry.

When he left, I hurried to put the cups and plates in the dishwasher, double-lock the door, and turn off the lamps. I started for the stairs, then went back and took the rose in its slender vase with me. I wasn't sure why.

I set the rose beside my bed, took a deep breath, and opened the drawer.

I sat on the edge of my bed to read, the white down comforter puffing itself into a nest beneath me. Already my heart was jittering.

Oh, God, tell me what to do! I'm safe here at home. But that girl, Belinda. I should have told someone right away. I will. I will tell, but they won't believe me. They'll think me delusional. I have to be careful.

I looked up from the diary. Oh, Lottie. I'm feeling what you felt. I understand. What did you do? Did you tell?

I don't want to go back into that awful hospital. I had reason to be out of my mind after Baby Joan's death, but my reasons were known only to me. And when I tried to kill myself, they didn't know about the nights and the terrible dreams, where I was shaking her, shaking her. . . .

That's the way it was at night for me, listening all over again to Kirsty moan. I know about the terrible dreams, Lottie. I covered my eyes with my hands, then made myself go on reading.

But I can't leave that imprisoned girl there with him. What if he does kill her? How could I have ever thought I loved him?

There was only one more page, but I didn't have the strength to read it right away. There was a strange buzzing in my ears, like angry bees. Did you save her, Lottie? You saved yourself. I think now you're trying to save me. You gave me your secret diary as a terrible warning so I could save myself. But can I?

I took the rose from the vase and held it close, looking into the flower's pure, warm heart, and I kept holding it as I read the final page.

What happened today seems like a nightmare.

I decided I had to tell about Belinda. I'd tell Reverend Maxwell. He'd tell the police. Maybe I didn't even have to get involved.

I went downstairs.

Father was reading the morning paper. He looked over the top at me. "Do you know a girl named Belinda Cunningham?"

My heart slammed in my chest. Belinda? Could it be the same one?

"No," I whispered. "Why?"

"Poor girl. She was about your age. She jumped from the gallery of St. Matthew's. Apparently, she's been grieving, something about a drowning she was involved in. She'd been missing for two months."

I couldn't breathe, and I slumped down onto one of the dining room chairs. Mother rushed to get me a glass of water.

"You shouldn't have told Lottie such a horrible story," she scolded Father. "Now you've gone and upset her."

I saw them exchange glances, and I could tell they were remembering the time after Baby Joan that I'd swallowed a whole bottle of Mother's sleeping pills.

I sat there, sick and despairing. I knew Belinda hadn't jumped from that railing. I knew it. Too late. I should have told. Too late, and two deaths on my conscience now. Baby Joan's and Belinda Cunningham's.

Will I ever be forgiven, in this life or the next?

I closed the diary. I was cold, cold, cold, and I pulled the comforter up around me like angels' wings. But my shivering wouldn't stop. I got all the way into bed, huddled into myself, my eyes wide open. Thinking, as Grandma's pretty silver clock on the dresser ticked away the minutes.

One thing was clear to me. Noah was using Kirsty and my need for forgiveness to lure me down into the shades below, the way he had lured Lottie with the promise of Baby Joan. The way he might have taken others and kept them prisoner. He was a ghost, moving invisibly, knowing every whispered secret.

I set the diary on the bedside table and laid the rose on top of it, the way you'd place a flower on a grave. Beside it, on the table, was a folded piece of paper. Had it fallen out of the diary?

I picked it up, opened it, and saw that it was the leaflet Donna Cuesta's mother had given me on our way into *The Nutcracker*. I looked vaguely at the words, my mind still struggling with what I'd learned from the diary.

And then the words weren't blurred at all. They jumped out at me, clear and sharp and horrifying. HAVE YOU SEEN THIS GIRL? And her picture—the long dark hair, the wide dark eyes. Donna Cuesta, who had disappeared, who had worn a serpent ring, who had met some mysterious person in St. Matthew's. Who had fallen in love. . . . Who had vanished.

Could she be down there, behind that wall, prisoner of a ghost?

I was shaking, terrified. Did I have to do something about this suspicion? Tell?

But what if I was wrong? It would be the way it was before. Everyone being kind but nervous around me because poor Catherine was obviously having delusions again. Ghosts and prisoners and murder.

I could show them the diary.

Well, Lottie Lovelace, that crazy old lady. It's the kind of thing she *would* make up. Hadn't she tried to kill herself once?

But what *could* I do?

Did I have to do anything? No. I could empty my mind of all that had happened here, the year I came to spend Christmas with my grandmother. I could go home to the safety of Chicago in three days. Till then I could stay away from St. Matthew's and Noah. I could be sick, maybe even go home early. Or . . .

I picked up the rose and held it against my face as I reread Lottie's words:

. . . two deaths on my conscience now. Baby Joan's and Belinda Cunningham's.

Will I ever be forgiven, in this life or the next?

If I didn't try to rescue Donna Cuesta, who might or might not even be in need of rescuing, would I ever be forgiven? In this life or the next?

It was like being given a second chance. A life I could save in exchange for a life I had ended.

It was almost morning. I'd lain awake all night. I went to the window and looked out. Still dark. The roof of the house across the street was garlanded with Christmas lights. They shone red and green, reflecting themselves in the palm trees and the leaves of a giant bird of paradise.

There wasn't a sound. No traffic. No dogs barking. I would have liked a dog barking, another creature awake like me. I had a decision to make. And only a little time to make it.

The Presence stood by his wall of ladies and talked to Lydia, his first and deepest love. He still loved her, after all these years, even though she was the one responsible for all his pain and heartache. She'd led him to believe she loved him when the two of them were in the youth choir. But she'd pulled away, screaming, when he'd pressed himself on her that night after choir practice. He'd tried to stop her with his hands around her throat, so intent on whispering his love for her that he hadn't heard the deacon come up behind him.

The deacon said afterward that he hadn't meant to bring the heavy candlestick down so hard on Noah's head. Noah heard him say that, because he wasn't really dead. He was dead, but undead. He could stand, but his body still lay on the green carpet of the sanctuary, blood trickling from his ears and his nose and his mouth. He could speak, and he did, but no one heard him. He'd told them he hadn't meant to kill her. He'd thought she loved him. But when he'd tried to touch her in an intimate way, she'd started screaming. He'd only wanted her to be quiet, so they could talk. He hadn't meant to squeeze so hard. They couldn't hear him as he explained to them what really happened.

He'd wanted to go to Lydia's funeral, but when he tried to leave the church, he'd found he was trapped there. When he threw himself through the open door, he was jerked back, like a cow on a tether. When he tried to climb through a window, his body could not make the movements happen.

The slow realization came that he was not to be allowed to leave St. Matthew's. It took weeks before he recognized that this life sentence was, in reality, a death sentence.

It took more months before he realized all his ghostly powers, before he felt and understood his forever loneliness and looked for someone to fill Lydia's place.

And now he almost had Catherine.

"She isn't you, my darling Lydia," he told the painted picture. "But I believe she is more like you than any of the others."

He walked beneath his ladies, smiling, speaking a word of love to each of them.

"My little wildcat," he said affectionately to Florence.

He stroked Donna's painted foot. "And you tried to escape, you rascal. I would have kept you longer. You were the best, so far. But after that, I couldn't trust you. You would have told. And I had to put you with the others. I had to hide you in a safe and secret place."

He stopped in front of the half-finished painting of Catherine. "I haven't completed your likeness yet. But you will see how I plan to honor you, as I've honored all my ladies."

He sat in his easy chair then and put on the CD of Sibelius. Finlandia. *He could feel in the music the forests and the lakes, the mountains and the snow that he'd never see. He closed his eyes. Sibelius would keep him company through the long, long night.*

FIFTEEN

I finally slept, and it was after eleven o'clock in the morning before I woke up. There'd been no dreams, bad or otherwise. I felt calm.

Birds chirped outside my window. Sunlight striped the floor.

I put on the pink robe, brushed my hair, and examined my thoughts again. Last night I'd made my decision. Did I feel the same way this morning? Yes. Was I still at peace with it? Yes.

Noah would be waiting at three. I'd be there.

I went downstairs. Grandma was sitting at the dining room table, which was covered with photographs. I stood behind her and smoothed her hair.

"Old pictures," she said, smiling up at me. "I thought you might like to see them."

"Great!" I was surprised that I was this lucid, this free from doubt. I leaned over the back of the chair and picked up one of the photographs. It was of a little girl with curly hair and dimples, knock-kneed on roller-skates. "Is this my mom?"

"It is. And here's your aunt Sharon. And look, here's your great-aunt Beverly with me. Weren't we hot? The boys called us 'the sizzling sisters.' Or sometimes 'the toothsome twosome.'"

I looked down at the two perky faces under the big flowered hats. "I can see why."

Last night, before I'd managed to get to sleep, I'd looked again at the blank, shining photograph that Lottie had taken. I'd stared at it, trying to see a shape, a shadow.

There was nothing, of course.

I'd turned it over and read "Noah" on the back in Lottie's writing, which I'd come to know so well. "The man who wasn't there," I'd said out loud, and now I thought, I hope the real Noah won't be there today.

But he would.

My stomach gave a warning cramp, but I willed it away. My stomach was not as serene as the rest of me.

Grandma held out another picture. "Remember the boy I told you about? The one who brought me the dandelion? Here he is."

I took the picture. "But that's Grandpa."

"Of course it's Grandpa. Did you think I'd let a fellow who was that creative and imaginative get away?" She smiled at me smugly and laid the picture tenderly on top of the others. "It's been seven years since he died, and I still miss him. We used to go dancing. I still dance with him every night when I dream."

I leaned down and kissed the top of her head.

"All right," she said briskly. "How about some break-fast?"

"Just some cereal, thanks." I took the Cheerios from the pantry shelf. "Oh, by the way, Collin asked me to go on a picnic with him to Tournament Park. We'll ride our bikes. There's a band playing Christmas music."

I opened the refrigerator to get milk so I wouldn't have to look at her as I lied, and I saw the plump little turkey defrosting for tomorrow. Christmas.

Grandma was beaming at me. "A picnic in the park? What a splendid idea." She stood, knocking over a couple of pictures, bending to pick them up. "I'll help you get the food together. Oh, and you know what? I have a back-pack somewhere. We can pack everything in that."

We fixed two thick ham and lettuce sandwiches. There were two winter pears and a small roll of goat cheese with herbs to go with them. She put the last of the cookies into a plastic bag, and two cans of juice into the freezer to ice up.

"If there's too much, there'll be someone around

who'll be glad to get it. There are always homeless people in Tournament Park. It just breaks your heart to see them." She sighed. "I'll go look for that backpack."

I rummaged around in the kitchen drawer while she was gone, searching for a flashlight. There was one, but its light was dim. I rummaged some more, looking for new batteries, but I couldn't find any. There was a red candle, though, and a dog-eared book of matches and a roll of plastic tape. I'd need that, too. I slipped everything into the pocket of my robe.

Grandma stowed the picnic carefully in the backpack, with paper plates and napkins patterned with holly leaves. She put in a block of ice.

I felt bad knowing that Collin and I weren't going to eat the food or even be together. But pretending to go on this picnic would give me all the time I needed. And he *had* asked me. That part wasn't a lie.

"What time is he coming for you?" Grandma asked.

"He isn't. We're meeting there." I glanced at my watch. "My gosh. It's almost one o'clock already. I need to hurry."

I ran upstairs, put the photograph in the diary, and wrapped them both in the paper they'd come in. I taped the package securely. On the front, I printed Miss

Lovelace's name and address. There was a small post office I'd noticed a few blocks from Grandma's. These had to go back. I'd given my word.

I dressed quickly in jeans and a black sweatshirt, the darkest clothes I had, and put on my running shoes. Maybe I'd have to run. The flashlight and candle and matches went in my pocket.

Before I left the room, I pulled my locket up from where it lay next to my skin, next to my heart. When I opened it, Kirsty's face smiled out at me. Friends forever.

"I'm doing this to make amends," I whispered. "I don't believe now that I am going to speak to you. But if I can save someone else, I hope you'll think it a fair return on what I did to you." I held the locket to my lips, then slid it back to where it had lain since the day I first got it.

When I came downstairs, Grandma handed me the backpack. I slipped Miss Lovelace's package in beside the food.

"Enjoy your day, sweetie," she said. "Be home in time for dinner." She smiled. "I like saying that. It's like the old days, when your mother went out somewhere in the afternoon. Having you around brings back so many good memories."

"I'll be home," I reassured her. But I knew the one who needed reassuring most was me.

The Presence looked around his room, making sure everything was as it should be for Catherine.

"I want you ladies to be nice to her," he told his wall paintings. "She's coming today. No jealousy, now. Eliza May, you did not look kindly on Donna when I first brought her here. No frowning when Catherine comes. I will introduce you all, and I want your smiles to stay in place."

He went to his table and picked up the note Catherine had left for him in the church and read it aloud. "I have to see Kirsty. Tomorrow. Here." He turned again to the paintings. "I'll leave this in one of the pews," he said, speaking to them collectively. He tried to do that as much as possible so there'd be no jealousy. So that they'd remember that he'd loved each of them once.

He held the note so they could see it. "Because of this, no one will question why she disappeared. Poor Catherine. She never could get over her guilt about her friend's death. I don't know exactly what happened to her that night or why she's carrying such a heavy burden. Unfortunately, she doesn't seem to have told anyone. Perhaps a little later she'll tell me, and we'll face it together. Meanwhile . . . "

He smiled appreciatively at his ladies. "You all helped me—by being depressed over your past guilts. There were questions asked, inquiries made, lakes dragged, woods searched, but in the end, there was acceptance. Sad girls. All of you so troubled. Who could blame you for disappearing and trying to find new lives? I tried my best to help you. You know that."

There was a can of apple juice on the table and two glasses, one of them for him, though he, of course, could not drink. He'd hold it up, empty, and click glasses with Catherine, and make a toast. "To us. To our future. May we have many long years together."

He frowned, remembering he'd hoped that for each and every new love he'd brought here, and look what had happened. But this one would be different. He wouldn't let himself remember that he'd thought Alice would be different, and Florence, and little Donna. He'd thought each of them would be different.

The serpent ring was waiting. He picked it up. The red eyes flashed, the gold band twined itself around his finger. "Well, now," the Presence said, content. "I think we are ready."

I cycled to the post office and mailed Miss Lovelace's package. She wouldn't get it till after Christmas. She'd wonder if I'd read it, if I believed it. I'd call her when this was over. If I got the chance.

At the block that came before St. Matthew's, I stopped. There were thick oleander bushes bordering a vacant lot. I pushed Grandma's bike and the backpack under them, pulling the branches around to hide them.

The old building watched me coming, its rose and gold windows flaming in the sun.

I checked my watch. Two-thirty-five.

He'd said to come at three. If I was right, he'd already be at the front office window, watching for me. He'd told me before how he watched me come all the way from the corner. Even then it had given me the creeps. It still did. But I was praying that was where he was right now, not suspecting I'd come from the other direction. I was basing my life on an assumption. But it was all I had.

The parking lot was empty. The afternoon before Christmas and no staff around, no cars to hide behind as

I ran across the empty space. What if he was watching from a back window and I'd figured wrong?

I ran as fast as I could for the shelter of the church wall.

The day I'd first come, Collin had told me that the back door to the church was sometimes left open. It *had* to be open now. I stood in front of it and touched the knob, which was warm from the sun and loose from so much turning.

It didn't open. I tried the opposite direction, leaned my weight against the door.

Nothing. It was locked, maybe because of the holidays.

Now what?

My breath was ragged in my throat. I should have expected this. Dumb, dumb, dumb.

Two-forty now.

I took a step back and looked up. An overhang sat like a cap above the door, under a vine covered with white blossoms that climbed the wall next to it. I'd felt a little secure under that small covering. Farther back like this, I knew I was exposed and vulnerable.

I checked my watch. Two-forty-three.

If I was going to get in, I needed to hurry.

Tilting my head, I saw that above the overhang was a small paned window. And it was open about two inches from the bottom. Ants ran up the vine in a straight line that could have been a shoelace unless you looked closely.

If the window was open a couple of inches, it could probably be pushed up further, enough so I could squeeze myself through. But that would take so much time. Maybe I couldn't even get up there.

I leaned my cheek against the smooth wood of the door and tried to think. I was going or I wasn't.

If Donna Cuesta was down there, I could set her free. If I couldn't free her, but if I found out for sure she was there, then I could call the police.

Or I could give up now. I'd be taking a chance on someone's life, leaving her a ghost prisoner forever, or until Noah became disappointed in her. The way he'd become disappointed in Belinda Cunningham.

I was shaking, pressed like a limpet against the door.

I made myself step back again and look up at the window. Then I took hold of the thick stem of the crawling white vine. It wasn't sturdy like a tree trunk, but when I tugged at it, it didn't pull away from the wall.

Two-forty-eight.

He'd wait a few minutes after three, still thinking I'd

come. But even so, I had hardly any time. If I was going . . .

I began the climb, holding the scabby branch, white flowers dropping like snowflakes around me. My other hand reached for the rough stone of the overhang and found it, so I could walk my way up the wall, up, up, till I was lying on my stomach across the small porch roof. Ants marched over my arms and hands. I thought I felt them in my ears.

I caught the window ledge, the splintery, unpainted wood tearing at my fingers. Now I was pushing the window, and it was creaking up, stopping and sticking.

Panic churned inside me. What if Noah heard the noise, came running, grabbed my wrists, pulled me in?

I lay there on my stomach, panting like a dog, my legs dangling, the white snowflakes falling lazily around me. I listened, but the only sound was the cawing of crows, fighting over something in the parking lot.

The window had opened as far as it would go. There were maybe fourteen or sixteen inches of space. Enough for my shoulders to squeeze through?

I wriggled, headfirst, terrified of being caught half in, half out, and fell with a thump on the wooden floor. For a couple of seconds I lay there, alert to any sound.

What if he'd heard that thump? Would I have time to squeeze myself back through the window?

There was nothing, not even the squawk, squawk of the crows.

I sat up, all of me hurting. I was in a small storage room filled with wooden chairs and music stands. Sheet music spilled from cardboard boxes against the wall.

I tiptoed across to the door and slowly opened it. Dusty steps led down, and I saw that I was somewhere behind the big pipe organ. My feet made no sound.

Now I could see all the way down into the quiet sanctuary. There were the candles piled in their baskets for tonight's midnight service. There was the row of scarlet poinsettias. I stood as still as a lizard, my eyes searching for any sign of Noah. He wasn't there, unless he had made himself invisible. I looked for a shadow, a stirring of the air, but there was nothing.

How could you outwit a man who wasn't there? What was I doing here anyway, taking this terrible risk? For what?

All right. For a chance at redemption.

Two-fifty.

I crept down the rest of the steps, across the front of the pulpit, and past the altar, crouching to make myself as small as possible. The arched door to the basement was closed. It squealed as I opened it and again when I closed it behind me. Instantly, I was swallowed up in blackness.

Lottie's diary words replayed in my mind. It was as if I heard her speaking them, a young girl, scared as I was. But she had thought she was going to meet a lover. If I met anyone, it would be a demon. "It was very dark," she'd said. "Dark as Hell must be."

"I smell evil," Grace, the little Native American girl, had whispered. Evil.

In the pocket of my jeans was the flashlight. I pulled it out. Its light was faint and pale, but it showed me the steps and the open space below. It wasn't fully finished down there. Part of the basement floor had not been excavated. It was outside earth, hard-packed, high as my head. The air was musty and dead as the inside of a tomb. My flashlight beam picked up the big stained armchairs, stuffing hanging out of them, broken pews piled one on top of the other, and an ancient piano.

I went farther down into the void, dark closing behind me. My light threw shadows on the back wall. I zigzagged the beam across the old plaster till I saw the big stone fireplace. I ran across to it and pressed my hands against the carvings. Something there slid the fireplace back. "Open, open, open," I whispered frantically.

The fluorescent glow of my watch face showed two-fifty-four.

Hurry! Hurry!

I leaned forward and put my mouth against the ice-cold stone. "Is anybody there?" My voice was so timid I could hardly hear it myself. But if Noah was close, I couldn't risk him hearing. Oh, please, don't let him be close.

My worn-out light showed me cobwebs, hanging like curtains. "Donna?" I whispered, louder now. "Are you in there?"

My flashlight went out.

But I thought I'd heard the smallest of sounds, like a gasp or a breath.

"Donna? I've come to get you out of there. Be ready to run."

I felt in my pocket for the candle and matches and clawed them out. On the third try, the candle lit, the flame wavering its white circle around me.

A minute after three.

Hurry! Hurry! Noah would wait only so long.

I moved my palms in circles against the carvings. Chips of broken stone stabbed at my hands. My shadow flickered on the dirty floor, shortened itself against the wall.

There was a coldness, a waft of frigid air behind me, and my heart jammed against my throat.

Noah was here. I knew it before he spoke.

"Catherine," he said. "I'm so glad you came."

"I was coming down to find you," she stammered.

The Presence heard the panic in her voice. Her eyes were wide and terrified. There were ants crawling on the front of her dark sweatshirt. White flowers like stars were stuck in her hair.

He reached out and touched her arm with his cold, cold hand.

"Welcome to my home, Catherine."

SEVENTEEN

I turned to face him. He wasn't there, but I knew his ghost self was.

Air hung frozen around me. The candle flame flickered blue. His voice came clearly from inside that chilled, empty space.

"I'm afraid Donna is no longer here, Catherine. And your friend Kirsty never was—as I think you've guessed. But stay, won't you?"

I heard the rumble as the fireplace opened behind me. I heard the grating sound of stone on stone, and I twisted around, afraid to turn my back on him. In a blink I saw the inside of his den, the big easy chair, the cot bed, the table, and, worst of all, the hideous paintings on his wall. Girls, all with long dark hair, their painted feet not touching the ground, as if they hung on gallows, all smiling their red-lipped gallows smiles and, oh, horror! There I was, on the end, half-finished in a painted blue dress I'd never owned, smiling my own disgusting, scarlet smile.

I jabbed back with my elbow and touched nothing.

He laughed, and I thrust the candle where I thought his face would be. There was a gasp, and I stumbled around where I thought he was, and ran, in a frenzy, toward the stairs.

The candle danced its hobgoblin light across the walls, and I glanced behind once to see where he was, even though I knew I would see only darkness and shadows and the opening to that ghastly room.

I stumbled against the claw foot of one of the abandoned chairs, pitched forward, fell into its torn softness. The candle jumped out of my hand, and there was a quick flash of flame flaring up on my right side.

I scrambled away from it, but suddenly everything was on fire, the chair, my sweatshirt sleeve, the right leg of my jeans. I began to run. Bad to run when you're on fire, very bad, but I had to, because the demon that was Noah was somewhere behind me, and that awful den was there, too, waiting for me.

I ran through smoke that made me cough and retch, that scalded my eyes and throat. I heard myself scream.

And then I was shoved from behind, I was on the floor of the basement, there was a coldness around me, over me, breathing on me.

Noah! He'd caught me. Better to burn up—

But he was rolling me over and over on the floor, slapping at my sweatshirt and my jeans, smothering the flames, and he was mumbling, "Lydia! Lydia, my love. I never meant to hurt you, never! Please believe . . . "

I was on my back, and I saw him, visible above me now, his body shaking. I saw the fire behind him, coming toward us in great hungry licks that caught him, the white shirt going up in flames, and I was crawling, dragging myself to the stairs, inching up them.

I didn't look back.

The Presence was on fire, a living torch. Fire! The one thing, the only thing in this world or the next that terrified him. He heard Mrs. Tibbs's voice: "You wet the bed again. You lied to save yourself from punishment. The fires of hell will consume you. You'll be turned on a spit, forever and ever." Then the swish and slap of the leather strap. The way it scorched his skin, blistered it, consumed him.

And now the fires of hell had him.

In an instant of crimson time he saw faces—Belinda, Florence, Eliza May—and he tried to say old remembered words. "I am heartily sorry . . . sorry . . . sorry." There were no words.

But he'd saved Lydia, his precious Lydia. She'd forgive him now. Would God?

Pain seared through him. Agony. He hadn't felt pain in more than a hundred years. Did this mean . . . ?

Through the torment, he had a moment of realization. He was human again. And he was dying.

Then there were no more thoughts, no more pain, just a wiping out of everything.

I was told that I crawled up those stairs and that the fire-fighters found me unconscious in the sanctuary. The fire, they said, had been confined to the basement. The Christmas Eve service had been canceled. The one on Christmas Day, too. I was taken to Huntington Hospital. I had second-degree burns, the skin on my arm and leg peeling and blistered. My throat and lungs were scorched.

It was a while before I was well enough to be questioned, my mom and dad and Grandma by my side as I told my story.

I can't honestly blame them, or the police, for not believing me. Who in their right mind would listen to such craziness?

It just happened to be true.

A body, charred beyond any hope of identification, had been found in the basement. "It's Noah," I whispered. "The ghost. He was visible, in human form, when he saved me. I've thought about it a lot, and I realize that it was because he'd become human again that he was able to die."

The police stared at me in disbelief.

I knew they suspected that I'd gone to the church to meet someone and that the meeting had gotten out of hand. Clearly, I was too ashamed to admit it.

Or perhaps someone had forced me into that base-ment and only the fire had saved me from rape, or worse. Why didn't I just tell? Well, they said, some young women didn't want to admit to rape, unfortunately.

"Weren't you supposed to be going on a picnic with the Miller boy?" they asked, probing me with their hard eyes and voices.

"I went to the church instead."

"Huh," the tall, thin officer said.

My parents and Grandma were appalled and fright-ened. A ghost? They looked at each other, but they wouldn't meet my eyes. Now she's seeing ghosts. We're back where we started.

I knew that my mom would be making appointments for me with Dr. West as soon as I got home. I could have told them about Lottie's diary. They could have gone to her with their questions. But it didn't seem fair to drag out the secret she'd protected for all these years. And for what? They'd only think the diary had encouraged me to imagine such an impossible story.

I felt calm and almost at peace. It might have been

partly the pain medications I was given day and night. But there was definitely a change in me. I'd been this close to death, but I was alive with a lot of time to think.

Noah! In the end, he'd given his life for mine, whatever life or half-life he possessed. He'd thought in that instant that I was someone called Lydia, someone he must have loved with all his heart. His need to save her, and his lasting love for her had been stronger than his evil.

But she was dead. And saving me would not have brought her back any more than saving Donna would have brought Kirsty back to me. If I'd died, would that have made Kirsty forgive me? Did I think she wanted vengeance?

I stared at her smiling face in my locket, and I seemed to hear her say, "Och, my foolish wee banty hen. Don't you know I forgave you a long time ago? It's you that needs to be forgiving your own silly self." She had been telling me that all these months. All I had to do was open my heart and listen. I knew her and the strength of our friendship. Why hadn't I known that?

We were back home before the four bodies were discovered, buried in the basement. They were identified as Alice Hart, Eliza May Little, Florence Peterson, all of them reported missing years before. And Donna Cuesta. I think I'd known she was dead the minute I saw her picture on the wall. Before that, I'd hoped and hoped that somehow I could find her. Now, reading her name in newsprint, I cried. I could see her looking out at me from the flyer. HAVE YOU SEEN THIS GIRL? CALL 1-800-THE-LOST. I could see her mother's sad, lined face.

Four lost girls. And how many more of the lost whose bodies were not in that basement? Belinda Cunningham, for one. And then there were the almost-lost, like Lottie Lovelace and me, Catherine Jeffers, saved in time.

It was accepted that the man who had been incinerated had killed all those girls. The burned-out room where he must have lived for many years had been searched and searched again. Nothing was left.

Who was the man? Who had lived in that blackened shell of a body? No one knew.

I knew.

The investigations dragged on, and although I was in faraway Chicago, I didn't escape them.

The Chicago police came to question me. Two detectives flew in from Pasadena. They were all kind and patient, but when I kept repeating the same story, they treated me the way you'd treat someone whose mind wasn't quite what it should be. I had nothing more to tell them.

As they were leaving, the second time they came, one of the Pasadena officers tipped something from a small envelope into his hand and held it out to me. "This was in the ashes," he said.

It was a ring. He let it slide around in his hand, the gold twisted serpent shining, its red ruby eyes sparkling under the lamplight. "Have you seen it before?"

"No," I whispered. "I think it belonged to Donna Cuesta. I was told she wore a ring like this."

I turned my head away from the officers. Lottie had worn it, too. I knew it was the ring Noah gave to his victims. Was it meant, this time, for me?

The detective let it slip back into the envelope. "Strange how the most unexpected things survive a fire," he said, and I nodded agreement. "Strange."

On a cold February afternoon, I called Miss Lottie Lovelace.

Her nurse answered, and I could tell by her small silence when I gave my name that she remembered me and that she knew some of the things that had happened.

"Just a minute, please," she said. "I'll see if Miss Lovelace wants to come to the phone."

I stared out the window at the naked elm trees, snow skimming their branches.

"Hello." Miss Lovelace's nervous old voice.

"Hello. I wanted to make sure you got the diary that I mailed back."

"Yes." I could hardly hear her.

"Good," I said. "I also wanted to thank you for letting me read it. For warning me." Tremulous and nervous myself now. "You saved me. You atoned for the baby—and Belinda." Would she understand what I was saying?

She began to cough, and I waited till the spasm passed, clutching the phone, listening to the thud of my heart. "He's dead, you know," I said. "He's the one they found burned to death in the basement."

"He was always dead," she said.

"But he's gone now. Gone forever," I told her.

"Are you sure?" Her voice was stronger now, clearer.

"Yes. He's gone forever."

"I am not so certain," she said and hung up the phone.

My hands were suddenly wet with sweat.

Grandma wrote that St. Matthew's was open for business again. The church itself had had little damage. Everyone sent love. All of her letters and e-mails were deliberately upbeat and cheerful, but underneath I sensed something more: a hesitation, an uncertainty, as if maybe she did believe my story. My grandma, who had lived long enough to know there are more mysteries in heaven and earth than any of us can even dream of. And that we all need to be delivered from ghosts and goblins and things that go bump in the night.

She was worried about my health, mental and physical. I kept reassuring her that Dr. West said I was making excellent progress. And that I knew I was. Though I had to work hard to keep the thought of those poor, dead girls from taking over my mind. The Lost, living in terror and dying in terror in that dark underworld where Noah reigned.

Sometimes she mentioned Collin.

"I saw him in the library," she wrote. "He sends his love, too."

Actually, he sent his love a lot, in e-mails and funny cards. Each one ended with the words, "Love, Collin." I knew that meant nothing. That's how everyone ends their letters, even to people they don't love at all. My dad joked that he once got an audit notification from the income tax people signed "Love from your friends at the IRS."

Collin's notes were short and stilted, but I looked forward to them more than anything.

I was back in school. "Everyone's being nice," I wrote to Collin. "If they think I'm a freak, they're hiding it. They're curious, of course. They quizzed me a lot, especially at the beginning, but they could see I didn't want to talk about it, and after a time they quit. They know I was in a fire and got hurt, and there was this creepy guy who tried to kidnap me and who'd killed other girls. That's all they know.

"At first, I was kind of a sensation. I think they're waiting till they sense I'm all better, and then they'll pounce. One of the girls told me the school principal talked to them before I came back, and warned them to be sensitive and not to interrogate me. I don't plan on telling more than they know already. Enough's enough.

"My parents are great. They're keeping me super busy, which I think is a part of their Big Plan. We hike in Lincoln Park. We've been to *The Lion King*, and next week we have tickets for a Bob Dylan concert. They're crazier about him than I am, but it will be fun. They don't ask questions."

Collin had asked very few questions himself. But I knew he would, sooner or later. Would I tell him everything? Would he believe me? That might be some kind of a test, and it made me nervous.

Sometimes in the night I'd wake up and think about Noah. I'd see him standing by my bed, the long sleeves of his white shirt rolled above his wrists. His curling dark hair. That brilliant smile. The grace of him, the charm.

And I'd sit up in bed and stifle my scream or shiver and shake and bury my head under the covers. Then I'd make myself visualize the photograph of him that Lottie had taken. Nothing but a blank. That's how I needed him to be. But on those nights, I knew I had a long way to go.

"He's gone now. Gone forever," I'd told Miss Lovelace.

"Are you sure?" she'd asked.

Of course I was sure.

And then it was spring vacation. Daffodils danced happily in our garden, and crocuses, purple and yellow, turned their faces to the first sun. My singed hair had grown back in. I was in my parents' bedroom, working on their computer, when I heard the doorbell ring.

It was Collin.

"My dad had a meeting in Chicago," he said. "I told

him I'd carry his bags." He was wearing the same dark pants and leather school jacket he'd worn the night we went to *The Nutcracker*. His blond hair still stuck up a little in back. "What a hunk!" Grandma had said. Grandma had an unerring eye for hunks.

My heart beat faster than fast. "I'm really glad to see you," I said. Jeepers! I hadn't meant to sound that glad!

He held out a flower—except it wasn't a flower, it was a dandelion, the fluffy kind that you blow on to make a wish. "This is for you. You can't imagine how hard it was to bring on the plane."

"I can guess." I felt as shy as he looked. He'd remembered Grandma's story, and I remembered, too.

"Are you going to blow on it now?" I sounded so dorky I was making myself sick.

"Should I?"

"Sure. I don't mind cleaning up the seeds."

"I'll help. But let's both hold it."

Our fingers touched on the smooth, milky stem. I closed my eyes, whispering in my mind the old-fashioned words that my grandfather had said to my grandmother all those years ago. "I wish that you would be my sweetheart forever and ever."

We both blew.

The gossamer seeds sailed like small parachutes around us, and the dandelion head was left bare on its stalk.

I thought that was a really good sign.

About the Author

Eve Bunting is the celebrated author of a wide range of books for young readers. Her novels for Clarion include *Spying on Miss Müller, Face at the Edge of the World*, and *Someone Is Hiding on Alcatraz Island*. She lives in Pasadena, California, with her husband, Ed.